Chapter 1

The sun beat down on me as I pulled my stuff from the back of our family's 1996 white minivan. I used to be so embarrassed to be seen in the minivan but now I felt sad leaving it behind.

"Are ya sure ya got everythin'?" my dad said.

"Well I have a lot more in my own car, but this is all that was in the van." I said.

"Ok, well I guess this is good bye, your brother and I have got ta be gettin' back on the road."

I looked over at my little brother and his thirteen year old pimpled face. He was standing on his knees in the backseat of the van, had a candy bar in his mouth and was waving bye to me. Looking at him and his buggy cheeks you would never know he was a technological genius. He loves comic books, particularly Spiderman and Wonder Woman and he spends all his weekends trying to recreate superhero powers for me through electronic gadgets.

I leaned in to give my dad a hug, but it was hard getting my arms all the way around his beer gut. My dad is a private investigator in Oregon and he's quite good at it. I used to help him out, but now he is going to have to recruit my older brother. He's in law school on the east coast and couldn't make the trip to drop me off at school.

I picked up my suitcase, blankets, pillows, and laundry hamper full of random stuff.

"Are ya sure ya don't want me ta help ya carry anythin' up them stairs?" my dad asked.

"No, I can do it myself, you two better be going, it's a long drive back."

The truth was I didn't want everyone in the dorms to see my dad. I wasn't embarrassed by him back home, but he blended in better there. Here, he was the overweight red neck amongst eager, over educated yuppies.

I stood on the sidewalk and waved good bye to the minivan as it rolled like an old whale backing out the parking lot. I walked up to the welcome table.

"Hi, my names Lennox Mar." I said to the girl behind the table.

"Hi! Welcome!" She said in an overly zealous voice. She looked down at a list of names. "Oh, this is exciting, you will be on the third floor of Homan Hall and I will be your RA! My name is Mallory and this is your planner, calendar of events, and informational packet! If you need help moving your stuff, you can find someone in a red shirt, and if you have any questions I'm here to answer them!"

I thanked her, took all my stuff and headed for my new dorm room. It was a warm sunny day with the smell of fresh cut grass and sunscreen lingering in the air. All around there were kids, carts, cars, parents, and students running around. Some students were crying as they said good bye to their parents. Others just wanted to know where the parties were. When I got to my floor, there was stuff all over the hall way and I gingerly tried to avoid stepping on anything, while I carried my stuff down the hall. I counted room numbers, 310...312...314...until I got to my room, 322. The door was already opened so I walked in.

I walked into a small square room with two beds, two desks and two closets. It had painted white brick walls and grey carpeting. There was a girl unpacking stuff on the left side of the room. She had long curly brown hair, a small waist and an athletically built body. She turned around when she heard the noise from the stuff I was carrying.

"Hi! My names Maggie Hansen! You must be Lennox Mar. Did you know we are both from Oregon? I looked you up on

Myface. I'm almost all unpacked. We got here yesterday. Do you need help with your stuff?" Maggie said.

"Hi. Yeah thanks. I have a few more things in my car." I said as I put my stuff down on my side of the small square room. I pushed my glasses a little higher up my nose. I don't actually need glasses. I wear them as part of my day time persona. During the day, I'm always trying to blend in and hide in the background as much as possible. I'm not someone who needs unwanted attention. "I parked right in front of the building."

We tried to avoid stepping on people's stuff as we walked out of the dorms. We had to wait for a few people to go by in the stairwell before we could walk down. Once we got to my car, Maggie stood there open mouthed.

"Wow, this is a cool car!" Maggie said.

"You have no idea", I thought to myself. We were looking at a black Audi RS 5 which is a nice sports car, but mine's a little extra special. My remote doesn't just lock and unlock the doors; it can make my car go invisible. It has a computer inside, has voice recognition, and it will drive it's self, but I thought that would take all the fun away. So, basically it's a smart spy car that was decked out by my brother.

"Thanks. The rest of my stuff is in the trunk." I said while opening the trunk and handing her some boxes.

When we got back to our room, I started unpacking. Mostly I just had to put some clothes in the closet and set up my computer and printer. I looked over at Maggie's side. She had lots of pictures of friends and family members, some old prom pictures, and a few Audrey Hepburn posters. There were cheerleading pompoms hanging from her bed, some stuffed animals sitting on her pillows, and everything on her desk was pink and orange, and perfectly organized.

"So why did you decide to go to school in California?" Maggie asked.

"I always liked California." I said. That wasn't exactly the truth. I came to school here, because my mom is the police chief in town. She left our family when I was six. My dad said the job in California was better than anything she could get in Oregon. My dad didn't want to move to California (he thought it was full of hippies, heaven forbid) and my mom thought her long hours weren't conducive for raising three kids, so she chose her job over raising my brothers' and I. Over the past twelve years I have gotten six phone calls and three letters from her. I decided to go to school in California to show her that I don't need her, that I turned out great. I want her to be forced to notice me. I don't want to be ignored any longer.

"I was a cheerleader in high school and now I'm thinking about joining a sorority. I'm a legacy to Delta Xi Alpha. Did you play any sports in high school? Are you going to join a sorority?" Maggie asked.

"No." I said. I really wanted all the questions to stop, the last thing I wanted was someone prying into my personal life.

There was a knock on our still open door. Maggie and I looked over to see a group of kids our ages all smiling and waving.

A kid with a green shirt and freckles said "Hi, my names Ryan. We are knocking on everyone's doors to introduce ourselves. Would you girls like to join us?"

"Yeah! That sounds like fun! Come on Lennox!" Maggie said.

"No thanks, I think I'll stay here and keep unpacking."

Maggie looked down at my mostly empty boxes and in a slightly disappointed voice she said, "Ok, well, I'll be back later and we can go to dinner together."

***

I feel scared. I am walking through a dark alley. There is a light breeze and I close my sweater I little tighter. The ground is covered in petals that reflect the high walls of the buildings on either side of me. I keep trying to focus on the dumpster up ahead to keep my mind off other things. I feel a sharp jab in my back that takes my breath away. My heart starts pounding, I know something is wrong. I am too scared to turn around, but when I hear footsteps running away from me I whip my head around. The pain in my back is getting worse and I am unable to move. As I am falling to the ground a man with dark hair, wearing a dark jacket and blue jeans runs out of the alley. I stare at the McBurger's and Old Blue across the street as I try to cope with the pain. I feel really tired and cold and I curl up in a ball, letting the pain take over my body.

I jolted awake and sat up. I was in my bed, in my dorm room. It was the middle of the night, and Maggie was sound asleep. I felt my back, but there was nothing there. I got out of bed and went over to my closet. I quietly pulled out dark pants, a dark pull over hoodie, and my favorite black combat boots. I put my blonde hair up in a ponytail and pulled a box from the back of my closet. I opened the box and took some red thick bracelets, a whip, a taser, a knife that I put in my boot, and most importantly, a mask I had bought at the Dollar and Cents store a few years ago. When I got into my car I put on all my stuff, and used the computer to look up places with both a McBurger and an Old Blue. Then I programmed my GPS to give me directions.

Putting my car on invisible mode so I could drive faster, I pulled up to the alley. I could see a woman lying on the ground with a small puddle of blood forming underneath her. I walked over and pressed my finger under her chin. She was already dead. I was too late. It happens, but not very often. My visions come to me at random times and there is no way to know when the event had or will occur. I used my bracelets to shoot a retractable web-like rope substance to the roof of the building on my right. I used the rope to walk up the side of the building. I walked over to the edge along the sidewalk and looked down the street for the man I saw in my vision.

I spotted him calmly walking past the Am-Pm on the corner. I backed up to get a running start and ran as fast as I could toward the edge of the building. I took a big jump into the air and shot a rope to the roof of the building across the street while thinking to myself (please work, please grip the building). My brother did make all my gadgets and I'm always worried they will fail while I'm free falling off a building. Fortunately for me they worked this time. I immediately shot another rope to the building on the other side of the street and just like Spiderman I swung from building to building all the way down the street. When I got to the guy I landed right behind him and wiped out my taser. Sometimes I'm too lazy to fight with someone. I dragged his body over to parking meter and used two zip ties to handcuff him to the pole. Then I called the police and told them the location of the woman and that the man who stabbed her was tied to a lamp post down the street, with the murder weapon still in his pocket.

Chapter 2

Maggie and I walked to the dining hall to get breakfast. I would have preferred to go by myself, but Maggie doesn't take no for an answer. The dining hall was in a building all by itself. Walking in we can hear loud talking and smell unrecognizable scents that one hoped were coming from something edible. A very nice older lady sitting on a high stool behind a small counter swiped our ID cards and asked us how we were doing.

We grabbed a plate off a rack and some silver-wear and walked around looking at the rows of food. There was lasagna, a salad bar, pizza, cereal, fried vegetables, and a rice vegetable mixture. I filled my plate and met up with Maggie by the tables. We looked for a table in a large room filled with people.

"You want to sit with the kids from our floor? They seem cool, nothing special, but at least we know them." Maggie said.

I looked around the room at everyone talking with their friends. I was having high school flashbacks to when I sat in the back of the cafeteria with some of the people in the chess club and kept to myself.

"I think I'll just find a table in the back, if it's all the same to you." I said. It wasn't that I didn't want to sit with everyone else; it was that they were going to ask me questions I wouldn't be able to answer.

"Ok, that's fine. I think that kid in the back corner over there is from our floor. He's by himself, maybe we can sit with him. Nobody should have to sit alone." Maggie said.

I doubted Maggie ever had the problem of not having anyone to sit with, but in that moment I was glad to have her with me, because I was too scared to talk to the kid sitting alone in the corner with his computer open and a pile of books next to him.

Maggie walked over to him and I followed behind her. I noticed lots of people looking at Maggie with jealousy and admiration and I felt kind of special that she was my roommate.

"Hi, I'm Maggie and this is Lennox, I think you are from our floor. Can we sit with you?" Maggie asked him.

"Hi, I'm Leo. Help yourself." Leo said.

"Are you working on homework already?" Maggie asked Leo

"Yes, I'm a pre-law major and I have a lot to work on." Leo said.

"Where are you from?" Maggie asked him

"The Bay area, what about you guys?" Leo asked

"We are both from Oregon. I'm from Salem." Maggie said as she looked over to me for my response.

"I'm from Portland."

"Oh cool, I've never been to Oregon but I would like to some day."

"So what do your parent's do?" Maggie asked Leo

"My dad's a lawyer and my mom's a pediatrician. What about yours?" Leo asked Maggie

"Oh, well, my mom's a teacher and my dad's a dentist. They really want me to be a doctor, but I want to be a writer. My parents don't approve of anything I do. They hated that I was a cheerleader and they really don't want me to join a sorority. My grandma and my aunts were all in the sorority, but my mom felt that they are an 'excuse for women to misbehave'. What are your parent's like?" Maggie asked Leo

Leo thought for a moment and then said "My parents are really supportive. I think they would be proud of me even if I told them I was going to be a stripper. My friends in high school told me it was the luxury of being an only child."

"You're an only child? I have an older brother. He's really annoying and totally my parent's favorite. I can't wait to gain some sisters through the sorority! What about you Lennox?" Maggie said looking at me excitedly.

"I have two brothers one's younger and one's older." I said, hoping they wouldn't ask more questions.

"You're a middle child! So what were you like in high school Leo? I bet you had lots of friends." Maggie said in a cute flirtatious voice.

Leo started to blush a little and said "No, I only had one friend and we were in orchestra together."

"Well I think that's better. I had lots of friends in high school, but I've never had a best friend. I always wanted to have that one friend who knows you better then yourself. That one person you do everything with." Maggie said as she stared off into the distance.

"Well I think I'm ready to go back to the dorms now." I said feeling awkward about the direction the conversation was heading. I didn't have friends in high school and I didn't mind, but I didn't want to share that. The last thing I wanted was someone feeling sorry for me. I fight crime for a living. I'm pretty sure I'm cooler than anyone else in this room right now.

When I got back to my dorm room I got a phone call from my mom.

"Hello Lennox, I see you are all moved into the dorms and are already causing problems. Did you tie up that guy to the light post last night? It looked like your handy work."

"How would you know what my 'handy work' looks like?"

"Look Lennox, I don't want you crime fighting. This is a dangerous city. Just focus on school work."

"I'll focus on whatever I want to focus on."

"Ok, hun. Well you keep your nose clean."

"Whatever mom…"

I hung up the phone. She knows exactly how to get under my skin.

I went to my beginning kinesiology class in the human health building. My professor is Mr. Morrison. He looks like your pervy Uncle who gets a little too handsy during Christmas dinner. He was going over the syllabus for the first day of class. It was pretty standard stuff so I let my mind relax and watched Mr. Morrison's mustache go up and down as he talked.

I see Leo walk into the dining hall. He is wearing khaki shorts, a polo shirt and carrying a very full backpack. Leo walks up to a pretty girl with long brown hair and a head band on. He shakes a little as he holds his tray of food. She stares at him with confusion. He utters, "Would you like to go out with me on Friday? There's a cool movie coming out." She laughs, shakes her head and sits down at her table. Everyone in the dining hall starts whispering amongst themselves, and laughing while watching Leo walk to the back corner. I felt a little sick to my stomach, and really sad for Leo.

"What is the policy on plagiarism? You with the blonde hair and glasses." Mr. Morrison said as he pointed at me.

I obviously didn't know the answer since I hadn't been paying attention. Fortunately, seeing the future isn't my only talent, I can also read minds. I concentrated on the teacher and picked up "expulsion".

"Correct." Mr. Morrison said with disappointment.

After class I went back to my dorm room where Maggie was talking about her sorority formal recruitment experience. She said that even though she is a legacy to Delta Xi Alpha she still has to go through formal recruitment where she meets all the girls in the different sorority houses.

I couldn't stop thinking about Leo and what I had seen earlier. I couldn't tell anyone about it without telling them that I have visions and that's a hard thing to explain to people. I also knew I was too shy to stand up for him in the dining hall. Maggie would stand up for him, but I couldn't tell her about what was going to happen. Maybe, I could suggest we go get dinner with Leo, so he's with us when it all happens. Maybe I can talk him out of asking that girl out.

"Hey Maggie, do you want to see if Leo would like to join us for dinner?"

"Yeah! That's a great idea; he's in my French class. I was talking to him in class today and apparently his roommate is some ex-football player and doesn't want to hang out with him. I can't imagine what that would be like. I'm glad you and I are friends."

I wouldn't have gone so far as to call us friends, but I was glad I didn't have to eat alone in the dining hall.

We walked down the hall to Leo's room and knocked on his door. A big guy with broad shoulders answered the door. He was definitely a football player. He looked Maggie up and down and grinned.

He said, "This is my lucky night. Are you looking for me babe?"

I stood there watching what was happening. Maggie took a step closer to him and stared him in the eyes.

In a calm, soft voice Maggie said, "No, pea brain, I'm here to ask Leo to dinner."

The football player didn't know what to do. He opened the door a little wider to reveal an open mouthed Leo sitting at a desk in front of his computer.

Maggie said over the guy's shoulder, "Hey Leo, you want to go to dinner with us?"

Leo leaped out of his chair like he had two seconds to get to the door before a bomb went off.

"Yeah..yeah..yeah… I want to go to dinner." Leo stammered.

On our way down the stairs we ran into some other people from our floor going to dinner and they said hi to us. Leo had a huge grin and I felt guilty knowing that in a few minutes he wasn't going to be smiling any more.

When we got to the dining hall, everyone dispersed with plates, looking for food. I lost track of Leo and quickly gathered my food and headed for the tables. The people from our floor were congregating at a table in the middle of the room. I walked over and sat down giving them a tentative smile. A second later I saw Leo walk over to the girl from my vision. I wanted to stand up and do something, but I didn't know what to do. I couldn't hit her, tie her up, or electrocute her. She turned him down, and he came over to our table visibly upset. Everyone tried making him feel better, but he put his tray down and walked out.

I could hear what everyone was thinking, and it made me really mad. I wanted to get up and yell at everyone. I really wanted to round-house kick a few people in the face. Instead, I sat there feeling bad for Leo. Maggie sat next to me and couldn't stop talking about how mad she was at the girl, for being mean to Leo. I suspected Maggie might have broken a few hearts herself back in the day, but I wasn't going to hold it against her. She obviously cared about Leo's feelings.

On our way out of the dining hall Maggie glared at the girl who had rejected Leo. She muttered some nasty words under her breath and clenched her fists. I kept walking out the door hoping Maggie would follow me, rather than trying to start a fight.

Maggie said to me, "I wish I had known that was going to happen. I would have stood up for him. One of my Aunts once told me, I have 'the power of beauty and with it comes great responsibility'. It wasn't until I was older that I understood she wasn't making a cheesy joke. I have the power of beauty. I can get guys to do whatever I want, I get free stuff all the time, and I have the power to help people feel better about themselves. I can advance someone's social status by being seen with them, but I can also break a lot of hearts. With beauty comes lots of people being jealous and lots of stereotypes and misconceptions about who I am. I think I could have helped Leo today, if I had been there earlier."

Having great power does bring great responsibility. Why did I have that vision of Leo? Was it my responsibility to help him, by telling Maggie about it? What are my responsibilities? What do my powers mean? Maggie was making me think about my powers in ways I hadn't before. My guilt over Leo was increasing, and I had to keep telling myself that he will be fine. My first week of college was turning out to be way more complicated than high school ever was.

Chapter 3

I'm at a party. It's loud, there's rap music playing and lots of people around. Occasionally I can hear someone cheer or yell. I have been drinking too much and am not feeling well. I am sitting in a dark room with rock band posters on the walls. I'm sitting on a bed with dark striped sheets and looking up at a guy with blonde hair and strong arms. I really like him and he's been flirting with me all night. I'm not sure what I'm doing in this room or where my friends are, but this guy makes me feel like I'm the only girl at this party and I don't want to let that go. He leans in and starts kissing me. His kisses started out soft, but quickly get rough. I can feel his hand move up my shirt. I don't really want him to, but I figure as long as that was all he did it was probably fine. I felt my bra come loose and he shifts his body weight pushing me down flat on the bed. I try speaking, but not much is coming out with his mouth over mine. I try pushing him off of me, but he pushes his weight down harder. He is kissing me on my neck and I yell out a faint "stop!" But his body weight makes it difficult to breathe or speak. I feel him undoing my pants and I try kicking. My heart is pounding, I am starting to sweat and the room is blurry. I smell whiskey and cigarettes and I feel a hand roughly grabbing my left boob. I try wiggling, hitting, kicking, biting, head butting, and yelling, but between him and the alcohol, it is useless. He gets my pants down, my underwear off and I hear his pants zipper go down. He pins my wrists down over my head, as he whispers "be a good girl and it will go quickly." His mouth engulfs my boob and he pushes inside me.

I let out a little scream, sat up and opened my eyes. I was completely entangled in my blankets, sitting on my dorm floor. I heard Maggie's bed creak and I looked over to see her peering down at me with complete bewilderment.

"Bad dream" I told her.

After breakfast I went to my drama class. I'm studying to be a personal trainer. It doesn't pay to be a superhero, so I needed to find a way to make a living by day. I figure if I was a personal trainer, it would make for an easy major. I would be done in four years, and I would get paid to get more physically fit, which would in turn help me be a better crime fighter. However, since I can read minds, I can cheat my way through everything. Yes, I know it's bad and will probably catch up with me when I'm not in school anymore, but I figured if I need to know the parts of a plant cell sometime in the future, I'll just look it up on the internet. Therefore, I decided to take a fun class like drama.

My drama teacher's name is Ms. Hayes. She's around the age of forty, with fiery red hair, piercing blue eyes and an elegant manor. She is mesmerizing. She has an elegant way of carrying herself and a very theatrical way of talking. Her voice is feminine, a little exotic and completely intoxicating. She is wearing a low cut, form fitting blue shirt with a black pencil skirt and a giant rock ring on the middle finger of her right hand. There is no wedding ring, but she has the undivided attention of all the boys in the class.

The class is full of mostly students you could tell did a lot of drama in high school, but there are also some taking the class to fill their schedule. Looking around at everyone, I noticed one guy in the second row with broad shoulders, a white t-shirt, buff arms and dark hair. He turned around and revealed a gorgeous smile, a strong jaw line and deep brown eyes that looked right past me to the blonde with the boobs popping out of her shirt sitting behind me.

I had a feeling I was going to like my drama class. I couldn't decide who was more fun to watch, the sexy body sitting in the second row, or the one woman melodrama being performed by a charismatic red head in the front.

***

I am standing outside and it's cold. It's the middle of the night and I'm nervous someone is going to see me. I've been watching this house for several days and I watched the family pack their car up this morning to go on a vacation to the beach. Staying low, I quietly walk to the side of the house. I use my sweatshirt to cover my hand as I punch the glass window. The window doesn't break. I look around and find a big rock. I throw the rock at the window and gingerly crawl through, while trying to avoid any glass.

I am there to steal anything I can carry out and sell for money. I really need a new dryer and those machines are not cheap.

I woke up, and sat up in bed. Maggie was sleeping under a big pile of blankets, so I got up, grabbed all my "crime fighting gear" and walked to my car.

In my vision, I had seen a street sign in the background that helped me find the house I believed was going to be robbed that night. The problem was I didn't know what time during the night the robber was going to strike, so I was glad I had brought some snacks to eat, while I waited. This time alone in my car also gave me time to think about the vision I had of a rape occurring. I was thinking the rape I saw probably already happened, but if I could figure out who the guy was, then I could find out when he was going to party again, and hopefully catch him the next time he tried to rape a girl. Guys like him don't just rape once.

Around two in the morning, I was getting sleepy, I finally saw a man in a hooded sweatshirt walking down the street. I knew right away that it was my robber. I waited until he walked around to the side of the house, before I quietly crawled out of my car. I heard him trying to break the side window, so I hid next to the bushes along the drive-way. I had an idea to go in through the front door and surprise attack him as he entered. I went over to the front door and not surprisingly, found it locked. I looked around for a key hidden somewhere, but couldn't find one. I was running out of time. The robber was already climbing into the house. There was a mail slot on the front door, so I tried reaching my hand through to unlock it, but couldn't get my hand far enough in. I made a mental note to ask my brother to make a gadget that picked locks for me, as I walked to the side of the house.

I climbed through the broken window and saw the robber staring at a flat screen TV mounted on the wall. I knew what he was thinking and a little part of me felt a little bad for him, but another part of me wanted him to get a legitimate nine to five job. I crept closer and kicked him between the legs. He doubled over and let out a yelp. I clasped my hands together and threw them upward as hard as I could under his chin knocking his head back. I kicked him straight in the stomach, knocking him down on his butt. I pulled out some zip ties and tied his hands together. I grabbed some rope from my belt and flattened his arms to his sides. I figured that would slow him down until the cops got there. I called the robbery in to the police and walked out the front door.

I jumped a few feet in the air when I looked down the driveway and saw Maggie standing there with her hands on her hips.

"You can kick the shit out of a guy, but you can't talk to people?"

"It's easier to be brave when I have a mask and combat boots on. It's like acting. It's a character I become."

"You have so much explaining to do."

"So do you. Were you sitting in the back of my car this whole time?"

"Yes, and you have no idea how bad I had to pee. The people in the blue house over there are going to have some great plants come spring."

"I could have sworn I saw you in your bed."

"I pulled my blankets over some pillows and hid in the backseat of your car."

"Alright, I guess I'll tell you everything on the way back. I want to get out of here before my mom shows up."

"Your mom? Why is your mom coming? Aren't you from Oregon?"

"Yeah, but my mom is the police chief here."

"Things are already starting to make more sense."

Chapter 4

It was late afternoon and I was sitting in my dorm room. The worst part about school is homework. It's the only time I can't cheat, so I actually have to look up the answers. Across the room, Maggie and Leo were working on homework as well. The two of them started out studying French together, but now Leo was tutoring her in Biology and editing her essay, for one of her literature classes.

I saw Leo and Maggie in a giant room with dim lights and lots of people. There were streamers, tables, balloons, and a big banner that said Delta Xi Alpha Spring Formal. Everyone was dressed in prom style dresses or tuxes. Maggie was wearing a long purple halter dress and her long brown hair was styled with soft waves. She looked stunning. Standing next to her was Leo in a classic black tux and a black skinny tie. Leo had a huge grin on his face and Maggie was bursting with excitement. Maggie looked like a princess and looked like she was having fun introducing Leo to all her friends, who found him adorable and charming. The two of them danced all night.

I smiled to myself, it was the first time, in a while, I had a vision of something positive.

"Hey, do you guys want to go get dinner?"

Maggie smiled at me, "yeah, I could use a break."

"Me too." Added Leo

***

I'm standing in a house. There are people everywhere, and it's so crowded I can hardly move. Some people in the kitchen are playing beer-pong and others are dancing to really loud rap music. I'm starting to sweat from the uncomfortable stuffiness of the house. I see a guy with blonde hair standing against a wall across the room. He's looking at me and I start to blush. This is my second college party and I came here with some people from the dorms. I have lost most of them in the crowd and I don't know who else to talk to. I keep hoping that the person who drove me here hasn't left without me. The guy from across the room starts walking toward me and someone yells "Mark! We need more beer!" The guy walking toward me looks over and yells back "There's more in the garage!" He continues to walk toward me. I can feel my heart racing; I'm not sure what to say to him. He invites me to his room where it's quieter and we can talk. We walk into his room and its dark except for a dim lamp by the bed. I notice the posters on the walls, as I sit down on dark striped sheets. Mark hands me a drink and sits next to me. I don't really want to drink, but I don't want him to think I'm lame either. I take a few sips and start to feel light headed. I don't know how long it takes to get drunk, I've never drank much before. A few minutes later the room is spinning and it's hard to keep my eyes open. Mark says something to me, but I can't tell what he's saying. He leans over and starts kissing me. He lowers me down flat on the bed and I lose consciousness.

I sat up in my bed. Thankfully this time I didn't scream and wake up Maggie, but I did need to stop this rapist, that I now know is called Mark. Maybe Maggie will know something with all her connections. I decided to ask her in the morning and went back to sleep.

***

In the morning Maggie and I had breakfast in the dining hall. We sat at our table in the back corner and I told her about the rape visions I had been having. I also explained my abilities to read minds and see things. Maggie took it surprisingly well and was extremely eager to help me in any way she could.

"Ok, well Mark is a pretty popular name and most of the parties I hear about are fraternity parties, which are technically in a house, but none of their houses have a garage." Maggie said. "So we need to find a house party in a college town that's being thrown by a guy named Mark."

"That shouldn't be too hard." I said sarcastically. "You're more sociable then me, maybe you could ask around today and find out if anyone knows of a party tonight."

"Do you know anything about the girls that got raped? Maybe your friend could help us find out who they are? Maybe they know where the house is."

"I know one girl is a freshman living in the dorms, but even if we find her we can't ask her about it. We aren't supposed to know anything, and she probably won't be thinking of the location, when I try to read her mind."

"Good point, I'm still new to all this. I'm doing my best." Maggie said.

I ate my cereal as I tried to think of any other details in my vision that would help us.

"Oh, I remember something! This really cute guy from my drama class was in my second vision. I bet he would know where the party was and when the next one is." I said.

"That's great! Maybe you can ask him about it after your class!"

"Um, well, actually, I'll probably never build up the courage to talk to him."

"Are you serious? We need to work on your social skills."

"Well, in the mean time maybe you could talk to him."

"Ok. I guess. What time does your class get out?"

"It's out at two this afternoon. His name is Sky, I think, and he's the handsome blonde with really buff arms."

"Got it! Two o'clock, blonde, buff arms."

All through drama class I listened to Ms. Hayes talk about the upcoming play she is directing. She was trying her hardest to get people to volunteer backstage and audition for parts. I was completely uninterested until she mentioned that Sky, (the hot buff blonde guy), had signed up to play the lead in the play. I wasn't going to pass up an opportunity to drool over him on my weekends, as well as during class. I was too shy to sign up for a part in the play, so I signed up for backstage work.

After class got out I waited for Sky to leave and then casually followed him onto campus. I looked around for Maggie and spotted her walking toward him. I sat down on a bench a few feet away.

Maggie walked up to Sky and introduced herself. "Hi, I'm Maggie, I'm a pledge for Delta Xi Alpha sorority and my sisters and I were looking for a good party to go to. I heard from some guys in my Chemistry class that there is a guy named Mark who throws some awesome house parties. You look like someone who might know where the best parties are. You wouldn't happen to know a Mark and where he's having his party would you?"

Sky was eating up what Maggie was serving and he said "yeah, I know a Mark. His parties are invite only, though. I know he's having another party tonight, but he won't let anyone in who isn't on his guest list."

"Do you know how we can get on the guest list?"

"No, I had a class with him last semester and suddenly I started getting party invites on Myface."

"Ok, well thanks anyway." Maggie said

"Sorry I couldn't help you and your sisters, but if you give me your number I can let you know the next time I hear of a good party."

"Yeah ok."

I watched Maggie give Sky her number and I felt jealous. After Sky walked away, Maggie walked over to me and sat down.

"Ok, so did you get anything? Did you read his mind?" Maggie asked.

"Yeah, his mind was mostly full of images of undressing you, but I did figure out where the house is."

"Ew, I didn't really need to know that, but yay, on the house. Just so you know, I gave him my number, in case we need him in the future. Not because I'm hoping he will call me. I know you like him, and I would never try to get in the middle of that."

"Thanks, but I doubt he knows I exist. So tonight we will go to the party. Are you sure you want to go with me?"

"Yes! This is really exciting, and I feel like we are doing something really important, which is cool."

"Haha ok."

"Do I need a costume like yours? If people see me with you, they might figure out who you are."

"If you keep crime fighting with me, then yes, but for tonight we would look weird hanging out in a party wearing masks. We need to blend in, so no costumes."

"Oh, ok, good idea."

Chapter 5

"What are you wearing?!" I asked Maggie, who was sitting next to me in my car wearing leopard print pants, brown heels, a tight pink tank top and hoop earrings. "I don't think that qualifies as blending in."

"It's a party. This is what people wear to parties, not jeans, a white v-neck shirt, tennis shoes, and hipster glasses." Maggie retorted as she looked me up and down.

"You kind of look like a cheap hooker, and what if we have to run? You won't be able to run in wedges."

"Maybe not, but we aren't on the guest list, so unless you have a better plan, I figure one look at me and the bouncer at the door will let us in. Guys rarely turn a girl away from a party, especially one who is dressed like a cheap hooker. Getting you in on the other hand might take some persuading."

The house was located across town in a gated community with fancy cars and manicured lawns. You could hear the music coming from the house a block away. There were cars lining both sides of the streets and people standing on sidewalks. There were a few people fighting over taxis and a line coming out the front door of the two story gray house in the middle of the street.

"There must be some good neighbors to put up with all these people and the noise." I said to Maggie.

"It doesn't even look like people live in the houses. They look dark inside, and there aren't any cars in the driveways."

"You're right! What a weird neighborhood."

I parked a few blocks away and we walked to the house. I approached the back of the line and stood behind a person dressed in pink tie-died pants, and a green shirt. I was letting my eyes adjust to the sight when Maggie tugged my arm.

"What are you doing? We aren't losers, we don't stand in line."

"But we aren't on the list either."

"Stripper outfit." Maggie stated while gesturing to her outfit with her hand. "Come on." Maggie said while motioning with her head for me to follow her.

We walked the length of the line, up the steps to the bouncer standing in front of the door. We moved aside as a girl stumbled out.

"Hi, my names Maggie and Mark said he put me on the list."

The bouncer looked through a list consisting of five pages. "What's your last name?" He said with slight agitation.

"Hansen, Maggie Hansen." Maggie stuck her chest out a little, pulled her shirt down slightly and smiled up at him.

"You're not on the list. Go to the back of the line."

"But Mark said he was going to put me on, maybe you could check again." Maggie said while biting her lower lip and batting her eye lashes.

With out even looking down at her the bouncer said, "You're not on the list. Go to the back of the line."

"Oh come on, just call him, he probably just forgot." Maggie tried protesting.

"This isn't a free for all party lady, if you aren't on the list you stand in line like the rest of the riff-raff."

Maggie's mouth dropped open a little and she turned around, grabbed my arm and walked the length of the line back behind the girl in the pink tie-died pants.

"I have never been called riff-raff before. I'm so insulted." Maggie said while crossing her arms. "And he called me 'lady'. Ugh, that makes me sound like I'm old."

"It's ok. We can find another way in."

"How?"

I thought for a moment and then I said, "Well, the house has a backyard, right? We can hop the fence into the backyard."

"The backyard probably attaches to someone else's backyard."

"You even said it yourself. These houses are weirdly quiet and empty looking. We can sneak into one person's backyard to hop the fence into Mark's backyard."

We walked around the block and followed the noise of the party to a big white house. There were no cars in the drive-way and all the lights inside the house were off.

"Ok, stay close," I whispered to Maggie, "We're going to sneak through the gate, hope there aren't any dogs, and hop the fence. Try not to talk in case there is someone home and they can hear us."

I walked up the drive-way keeping a watch for motion sensor lights or cameras. On the side of the house was a tall wooden gate with a cord dangling down. I slowly pulled the cord and slipped through the gate, followed by Maggie who was doing a weird exaggerated walk to keep her heels from making noise. Maggie slowly shut the gate behind her, while I cautiously looked around the corner of the house. There were no people, no lights, and one dopy looking golden retriever.

The dog slowly walked over to me, sniffed my hand and walked away while stumbling over its own feet. I waved my arm indicating that the coast was clear and for Maggie to follow me. Staying low, I ran across the yard to the back fence where I could clearly hear the party. Looking behind me I saw Maggie prancing across the lawn and keeping her eyes on the dog.

Through a hole in the fence line I found a tall tree surrounded by bushes, in the right-hand corner of Marks lawn. I followed the fence line to the corner and peaked over the top of the fence. Most of the people were either inside the house, in the pool or surrounding the bar on the other side of the yard. This was the perfect spot for us to hop over without being noticed and quickly blend into the crowd.

I whispered down to Maggie who was sitting with her back against the fence. "Ok, how good are you at hopping fences? One of us can boost the other over, but the last person is going to have to get creative."

"Well, I was a cheerleader, but I was at the bottom of the pyramids. I can hoist you over the fence, but I might not be able to climb over after you."

"Ok, then I'll give you a boost over and I'll follow after."

At that moment the dog wondered over to sniff some flowers. Maggie stood up and pressed herself flat against the fence.

"What are you doing?" I asked her.

"Shhhh… the dog is coming over; I'm hoping he doesn't see me."

"Maggie, he's hardly a guard dog, look at him, he's chewing on a dirty sock. Don't tell me you're afraid of dogs."

"I'm afraid of dogs."

"You're kidding me right?"

"NO! I got bit by one as a kid. I'm so scared of them."

"Ok, come on. I'll boost you over the fence."

I clasped my fingers together to form a cradle. Maggie took her heels off and chucked them over the fence into the bushes. She grabbed onto the top of the fence, put one foot in my hands and whispered "1…2…3!" I pushed her right leg up as she swung her left leg over the fence. She straddled the top of the fence line until she could get her right leg over and then she disappeared on the other side of the fence and fell into the bushes.

I stood in the corner where the two sides of the fences came together. I put a hand on one side, the other hand on top of the fence Maggie had just climbed over. While pulling my body closer to the fence with my arms I pushed against the fence with my feet. I had one foot on either side of the fence and walked my feet up. Unfortunately, I wasn't strong enough to also get my butt up, so I started dangling upside down. I looped both legs over the fence and ignoring the pain of the wood jutting into the back of my knees. I curled my head toward the top of the fence and pushed myself up to a sitting position on top of the fence. I looked down at Maggie, who had her palms together and her hands up in the air to cradle my butt as I came down. I turned around to face the house we had just snuck past and saw the dog peeing on the spot Maggie had been sitting. I lowered my butt into Maggie's hands and let go of the fence. We learned Maggie doesn't have super strength, when we both fell backward into the bushes, me on top of her.

We peaked around the tree to see if anyone had noticed and nobody had, so we stood up and crawled out of the bushes.

"We got in! We're in!" Maggie said.

"Alright you look for Mark, and ask around if you need to. Send me a text when you find him. I'm going to go look for the girl."

Maggie didn't even let me finish before she was off talking to a group of people. I decided to walk the perimeter outside, and then walk through all the rooms inside. There were a lot of people and I was picking up a lot of words from people's thoughts. There are times when I am glad I can read people's minds, but then there are other times when I feel like God getting inundated with a giant medley of prayers. Sometimes I don't want to get inside a person's head. In high school I decided to try one of my dad's beers and it quieted all my thoughts. Alcohol prevents me from hearing what people are thinking. I can only hear what they are saying and it also stops my visions. Right now I thought maybe a few sips of alcohol would quiet some of the thoughts I was picking up, and help me concentrate on finding the girl.

I walked over to the bar and asked the bartender to hand me something sweet. He mixed some stuff together and handed me a red plastic cup. I tasted the drink and it tasted like pink lemonade. I was still picking up a few thoughts and most of them were thinking about sex or drinks, and some people had a lot of drama going on. I didn't see the girl outside and the people in the hot tub were giving me weird looks, while I stared at them trying to make out their faces.

I headed inside the house. There were a bunch of people talking in the living room, beer pong in the kitchen, King's cup in the dining room, a long line to the bathroom, and lots of people going up and down the stairs. I looked along the living room wall where the girl in my vision had been standing, but she wasn't there.

I walked into the kitchen and almost got knocked over by a guy trying to catch a ping pong ball. I got some dirty looks, so I decided to move on. The King's cup game was ending and the guy drinking the King's cup was starting to throw-up. I moved on over to the bathroom line. I didn't see the girl, but I heard lots of people shouting through the bathroom door for someone to 'stop giving blow jobs'. I wandered up the stairs and saw things going on in the bedrooms that can never be unseen. Nobody looked like they were in trouble and I still didn't see the girl, so I went back down the stairs. I was almost to the bottom when I saw the girl walk by. I quickly pushed my way through the crowed to follow her.

She stood in the kitchen and watched the beer pong game. I leaned against a wall, and kept an eye on her. I looked around for Mark and saw him walk outside. At that moment someone holding a tray of little cups with gelatin in them walked by handing the cups out to people; I was hungry so I ate one. A few minutes later a girl walked by and handed me a red cup. I had already emptied my first cup, so I took the new one.

The girl started playing beer pong. I checked my phone to see if I had gotten a text from Maggie. She had texted to say she found some people, who told her Mark has a party two times a month. He's a rich kid who sends all his neighbors on vacations a couple times a year to keep them from calling the police on his parties.

After the girl lost her beer pong game she went outside, so I followed her. I saw Sky outside talking to some girls. They were laughing and flirting. I was feeling a lot braver and more sociable than when I had first fell into the party.

A tall guy standing next to me asked me where I got my glasses. I told him I found them online and that I was from Oregon, but that I was really liking California and that I was mad at my mom, but I really missed my dad and that my classes at school were easy, but I was starting to wish I had chosen to study something that really interested me. He started talking to a girl standing in front of him without responding to me. I felt a little hurt, but I wasn't there to make friends.

I spotted the girl going back inside. I followed her in and saw Sky playing beer pong. He was winning. The girl with the gelatin cups walked by and I grabbed a couple more. I don't know why she was handing out gelatin at a party, but I was still hungry and the gelatin tasted good.

The girl walked through the house and out the door with a group of students. "Dame it" I thought to myself, my vision was for a different night. I called Maggie on my cell phone.

"Hey girl! Where are you? Mark is in the hot tub and I'm watching him from the second story, but I haven't seen you all night!"

"I'm downstairs. The girl from my vision just left. It's not happening tonight."

"Oh good, I'm tired and really hungry!"

"Yeah, I'm starting to feel kind of sick, let's go back to the dorms. Meet me by the front door."

I was feeling a little unstable so I leaned against the wall. Maggie came running over and gave me a big hug.

"Hi friend!" Maggie said to me.

"Hi. Let's go." I said back.

We walked out the front door and the security guard looked at us and said, "Hey! I didn't let you guys in!"

"Yet we've been in there for hours." Maggie said with a lot of attitude.

"Maggie focus, I don't remember where we parked. I don't recognize anything."

"Don't panic I think we parked two or three blocks away. Oh my gosh, I need to sit down for a minute, my feet hurt."

"I want Taco Barn. Right now." I said.

"Ok, ok, princess, we'll keep walking."

Two blocks later we found the car.

"Have you been drinking?" Maggie asked.

"Yes, I had a drink or two and some gelatin."

"You had a few drinks and gelatin shots? I had one drink and two gelatin shots. I think that means I drank less than you, so maybe I should drive."

"Ugh, ok, I guess that makes sense. We can make the car invisible, so we won't get pulled over, but it won't be helpful if we hit someone."

"I got it. I have driven a car before."

Ten minutes later a neon Taco Barn sign appears.

"Taco Barn!!" I yell out.

Maggie swerves, narrowly missing a car.

"Don't yell in a moving car! I see the Taco Barn, but the car is also invisible, so how do you plan on going through the drive-thru?"

"Oh I didn't think about that. Find an alley and we will switch the car back to visible."

Maggie drove a few feet and suddenly veered to the left. "I see an alley!"

"Oh crap, geez Maggie, careful!"

"I didn't want to miss the alley."

"I think I might puke. I need to get out of the car for a minute. Don't touch any buttons."

I stood in the alley for a few minutes taking deep breaths. I heard the car door shut and when I turned around the car was gone.

"Maggie, that's not funny!" I stuck my hand out to feel for the car, but couldn't feel anything. I took a few steps forward and still couldn't find the car.

I tried walking down the alley a little with my hands out. "Maggie, come on. You better not touch any of the buttons! I'm hungry. I might throw-up. I think my right butt cheek is numb, and it's cold. Let me back in the car!"

"Beeeeeeep beeeeeep." I heard my car horn go off in two long honks.

"Maggie I'm not playing Marko Polo with you."

"Beeeeeep beeeeeep." The car sounded like it was a few feet away.

I started walking with my hands out and yelled "Marko!"

"Beeeeeep beeeeeeep."

Some flames started shooting out in the middle of the alley and I knew Maggie was playing around with the buttons in my car. I carefully walked toward the flames not wanting to get burned. When I got closer the flames disappeared.

I yelled again, "Marko!"

"Beeeeeep beeeeeeep."

I was walking around the alley with my arms out when I heard a pop noise and Maggie suddenly appears skidding down the alley still attached to her car seat.

"You pushed the buttons." I said to Maggie as she slid closer to where I was standing. I put my hands on my hips looking angry.

"What just happened?" Maggie said excitedly with a grin on her face.

"You hit the eject button and the car shot your seat out. Put the seat back in my car so we can go home."

Maggie got up and ran for the car; I felt sick and couldn't run very fast. Maggie found the car because the car door was open. The inside of the car is visible looking through the open door. She got back in before I could reach the car and once again I couldn't find it.

I yelled, "Marko!"

I heard, "Beeeeeep beeeeep!"

I heard something hit the dumpster in the alley and I knew it had to be the car. I ran over to the dumpster and felt my car. I walked around until I felt a door. I got the door open and climbed in. Maggie was laughing hysterically in the front seat.

"You are so dead Maggie! That's the last time I let you drive my car and you better not have dented it!!"

"Ok…Ok…. I'm sorry… hahahaha I just wanted to see if your car was actually invisible. Hahaha you should have seen yourself!"

I got in through the back seat so I had to climb to get to the front seat. "Let's just go to Taco Bell now!"

Twenty minutes later we safely pulled into the dorm parking lot. I was feeling a lot better after inhaling a burrito.

***

I had a rough morning. I skipped my kick-boxing class to sleep in a little longer. My mind reading abilities were back at full force, but I was glad I avoided having any visions last night. Sometimes I need a full night's sleep. Not that I felt well rested or anything.

In the afternoon, I went to my drama class. I made sure I was wearing a cute outfit, I also straightened my hair, because I never know when Sky might notice me. When I walked into class I could tell something was wrong. Ms. Hayes wasn't in the classroom and everyone was talking and looking around. It's not abnormal for a professor to be late to class, but I had an unexplainable feeling that this was more than Ms. Hayes just running a few minutes late. Sky was sitting in the front row with a pair of sunglasses on. I stood in the front of the classroom and had a strong urge to check the drama stage. It wasn't a vision just a very strong feeling.

I turned around and walked out of the classroom. I headed down the hall until I reached the door leading into the auditorium. I felt a knot in my stomach. I was hoping I wasn't going to find anything when I opened the door.

I slowly pushed the door open and looked toward the stage. My stomach dropped, I almost wet my pants a little and I suddenly wasn't sure what to do. Ms. Hayes's body was dangling over the drama stage by a noose. I walked closer and could see her blank eyes staring widely at the corner of the stage. Her body swayed a little in the breeze of the air conditioner. I felt sick to my stomach. I had seen dead bodies before, but I've never looked into the lifeless eyes of a person I knew. I really hate seeing dead bodies. It takes a long time to desensitize yourself to something like that. Yes, I'm a crime fighter, but I have morals. I don't kill if I can help it. Otherwise, how am I any better than the person that has killed? I believe in the justice system.

I pulled out my cell phone and called the murder in. I stuck around to talk to the police, although, I didn't have much to say. My mother was there, but we both avoided each other. Sky was sitting in the back of the auditorium watching them take pictures of the crime scene. He looked like he might have been choking back tears and I thought it was sweet coming from a man who has a tough disposition.

Since class was obviously canceled for the day, and a media ring was starting to form, I decided to go back to the dorms and meet up with Maggie.

Chapter 6

I walked into my dorm room and found Maggie watching TV shows on her laptop.

"Hey Maggie, I could really use some comfort food right now. You want to go with me to the dining hall?"

"Sure, I could use a food break."

We walked into the dining hall that was mostly empty. It wasn't a usual time of day to be eating. We grabbed a bunch of food and sat down at our table in the back corner.

"Did you hear about my drama teacher yet?" I asked Maggie.

"No, I haven't gone to class all day. I wanted to sleep in after last night."

"She was murdered. I showed up for class and found her hanging by a noose, above the drama stage."

"You didn't have a vision of it happening?"

"No, alcohol keeps me from having visions, or being able to read people's minds."

"Do you think you could have prevented the murder if you hadn't been drinking?"

"I don't know. I don't have a vision of every crime. There's no time frame between when I have the visions and when they occur, as we learned last night. I have no idea why I see some crimes happening and why I don't see others. If I could have prevented it, then I owe it to her to find her murderer. I have noticed that dead people can send me details of their murders in my visions. Hopefully, Ms. Hayes will reach out to me and send me useful visions about her murderer."

"Well, every great superhero has a sidekick, so I think I should be your official crime fighting partner. You will need someone to watch your back. Also, I love puzzles and I watch a lot of crime shows, so I might be able to help you solve the murder."

"Do you have any cool talents, or secret super powers?" I said half joking.

"I was a cheerleader, so I am pretty flexible and athletic. I took kick boxing and I know some self-defense…oh, and I don't know if it's helpful, but my brother taught me how to pick a lock."

"That's really helpful, actually. That's one thing I've always wanted to be able to do, but I never learned how."

"Awesome! Looks like you just got yourself a sidekick!"

I smiled, whether I liked it or not, I just got myself a friend, and as far as friends go, Maggie seemed like a pretty kick ass one.

"If we are going to fight crime together we need secret identities. People can't know who we are and they will figure it out if we call each other by our names." Maggie said.

"You're probably right. I just feel a little silly using a fake name like Batman, Spiderman or Superwoman."

"I can promise you, I will never let us become as ridiculous as Catwoman. There is no way you can do anything in tight pants and stilettos. Every girl knows heels hurt your feet after thirty minutes. They get stuck in cracks and grates, they sink into grass and make lots of noise when you walk. Don't even get me started on the tight pants." Maggie said.

"Haha, well I guess that makes me feel a little better. What are we going to call ourselves?"

"Um… well I guess superheroes got their names from descriptions of their powers. I never read comic books, but it seems to me if we describe our power and add a color or man or woman after it then we have a superhero name."

"I never read comic books either, but that sounds good to me."

"So your powers are psychic and mind reading. Those both have to do with the brain, but you also use webby rope like Spiderman and you can fight. So maybe something like crouching tiger, or webby ninja?"

"Those are terrible names! Let's search different words for psychic on the internet, since that's what I use the most."

I pulled out my phone and searched words on the internet.

"Oh! What about 'Mystic'?" I asked.

"I like the word but we need something else to go with it - like Mystic girl, or Flying Mystic. Do you have a favorite color or animal?"

"I guess my favorite color is blue and I like dogs."

"No, we need a color that sounds cool, or an exotic animal. What's your favorite animal print to wear?"

"Sometimes I wear cheetah print, but never zebra, and I like giraffe, but it's hard to find things made in giraffe print."

"Now that I think about it, giraffe print really isn't that popular. I like the sound of cheetah, though. How do you like the sound of Mystic Cheetah?" Maggie asked the last part with her hand in the air, as if she was picturing the name written across a billboard.

"No, I don't like that. Cheetah has nothing to do with my powers. I'm not exceptionally fast, or anything. Maybe we could find a Native American name. My family is part Black Feet Indian."

Maggie typed some stuff into her phone and after a few minutes said, "What about the name Koko? It says on this website that it means 'night' and that people with this name are usually mystics, philosophers, scholars, and teachers. It says, when these people are presented with issues, they will see the larger picture. That sounds like you."

"I like it! Now what are we going to call you?"

"Well, I love the color pink. My high school mascot was a wolf, and I love pizza."

"You aren't signing up for a dating sight. None of those, except maybe wolf are useful."

"You're right! So I need a word for athletic."

"I already up words for lock picking. I think that's your strongest characteristic. What do you think of the word breach?"

"I think it sounds cool."

"So maybe Breaching Wolf, Breach Girl, or Lady Breach."

"No, I don't like those."

"Ok, maybe we can use the sorority?"

"Oh! What about Omega? It's at the end of the Greek alphabet and since I don't actually have a real superpower, it seems fitting to be at the end. Usually people use Alpha or Beta."

"I like Omega Girl. It has a nice ring to it."

"Omega Girl and Koko it is then."

"What are we going to do about costumes? What should our masks look like?"

"What about what we already wear, or something like in the comic books?"

I thought for a moment, as I finished eating my tomato soup. "Do we have to wear the same thing?"

"No, I guess not."

"I want to blend in with the dark. Our outfits should be black, comfortable, stretchy and practical."

"I'm thinking yoga pants, black tennis shoes, and black zip up hoodies, but we'll have to pack gadgets underneath, since we'll be missing a belt."

"That sounds perfect, except what about in the summer? I don't want to be in a hoodie, and I've always fought crime in my boots. They make it easier to kick ass."

"Alright in the summer we can both wear cool wicking long sleeve shirts, and I'll wear the yoga pants and tennis shoes. You can wear stretchy black jeggings with your boots."

"I like it!"

"Me too! I'll start putting the outfits together right now."

***

Sitting in my kinesiology class I could hear people whispering about Ms. Hayes's death. Everyone was still shocked by the events, and lots of rumors were floating around campus on who killed her and why. Rumors were sometimes based on truth, and could serve as a good place to start looking, so I listened in case I heard something I thought could be useful.

While I watched the professor write notes on the board, I ended up standing in front of a bank. I'm getting excited and addicted to the adrenaline rush of what I am about to do. I look up at the bank sign on the building. I had planned this for three days, and now it was happening. I know where the security cameras are located, and I have a plan to blow out the door to the money vault. This is going to work, because I have it planned so that I can get away, before the police arrive.

My heist was interrupted by someone's thought. It was a thought about Mark's next party. He was having another party to celebrate the football game that was happening that night. I really wanted to go to the football game, but between Mark's party and the impending bank robbery, I was going to be too busy tonight.

As soon as class got out I ran to the dorm. Well, I didn't run, because I would look ridiculous. I briskly walked to the dorms. I was excited to find Maggie sitting in our room.

"Maggie, I had a vision of a bank robbery, and I found out that Mark's having another party tonight."

"I heard about Mark's party, and my sorority got on the list, so it shouldn't be a problem to get in this time."

"Well, I don't know when the robbery is going to happen and I'm not sure, which bank is going to get robbed, I can't stake out a bank and go to a party in one night. Also, I haven't gotten anywhere with Ms. Hayes's murder."

Maggie stared at the floor for a few minutes and then looked up at me with a very serious face. "First, you haven't noticed, but the bag on your bed is your new superhero outfit. Second, we need more help, and I think we should include Leo on everything. Leo is really good with computers and he's super smart. We are going to need more than just your visions and mind reading to help us solve the murder. Third, I'll go to the party, since I'm on the list and I'll call you if Mark takes a girl to his room. With you in one place and me in another we are going to need a third person to have both our backs; someone who can keep in-touch with both of us, in case something goes wrong. I think we need Leo."

"Ok."

"Really? You aren't going to argue with me."

"Nope, you're right and thanks for the clothes. I love the mask. It looks cooler than I thought it would. Let's bring Leo in here right now, and tell him everything."

Maggie pulls out her phone and calls Leo. A few seconds later there's a knock at our door. I felt both nervous and scared, for his reaction.

"Hi, what did you want to talk to me about?" Leo asked with a nervous look and fidgety hands.

Maggie shoved him over to a desk chair. "Why don't you sit down, this won't take long, but you might be shocked by what you hear."

I sat across from him on my bed, and glanced over at Maggie, who gave me a reassuring smile back.

"There is no easy way to say this, so I'm just going to come out and say it. I have psychic visions, sometimes I see random moments in the future, but mostly I see crimes occurring. I can also read people's minds. I started having visions as a kid, and didn't know what to do about them. But after helping my dad with his private investigative work, I decided that I could help the police by catching bad guys in the act of committing crimes. Sometimes, I take a video or picture of them committing an act and send it in to the police, but other times I just tie the person up next to the scene of the crime. My mom is the police chief here and I don't get along with her, but I love fighting crime, largely because she doesn't approve. Maggie found out my secret when she hid under a pile of my stuff in the back seat of my car one night, when I stopped a home burglary. She is now my official sidekick, with a superpower of lock picking and beauty. We currently have more crimes to prevent, plus a murder to solve and we can't handle it all. Maggie and I wanted to let you in on our secret, in hopes that you will join us to fight crime."

There was a long pause as Leo stared at me open mouthed, and Maggie and I stared back at him, waiting for his reaction.

After several minutes Leo took a deep breath and said, "That is the coolest thing I have ever heard! I love superheroes. I mean who doesn't! I would love to work with you guys!"

Leo was practically jumping out of his seat with excitement. I caught him up on the rape, the murder, and the robbery. He agreed to see what he could dig up on Ms. Hayes. We also had fun trying to come up with a superhero name for him. After thirty minutes of arguing, web searching and laughing we came up with The Blue Sleuth.

I pulled out mini long distance walky-talky's from my closet for everyone. "These are to always be kept on you at all times, and always be left on. They come with a small cordless ear piece. We will set them to the same channel, and if anyone needs to contact one of us, always use our code names. The sound comes through the ear piece, so you are the only one that can hear what is being said. Does everyone understand their gadgets, and responsibilities?"

Everyone nodded, Leo decided he should move into our room, so his roommate won't catch on to our escapades. We agreed. I told him he could set his computer at my desk, since I never use it anyway.

Maggie and I gathered our outfits and went to the car. Once we were in the car we made it invisible and changed into our outfits. I had a spare party outfit in the backseat, but put on my new Koko outfit for the bank. Maggie had her Omega Girl outfit in the backseat, but was dressed in a cute dress with leggings for the party.

I drove Maggie to Mark's house and dropped her off. I used the computer in my car to look up banks and found twenty. Using street view I looked at all twenty, until I found the one that looked like the bank in my vision. I programmed the address for the bank into my cars' GPS. I drove to the bank and parked in the parking lot leaving my car as invisible. I reclined my driving seat and sat back to wait.

Four hours later I was almost asleep and half way through my third movie, when I saw a guy walking down the street in jeans and a dark sweatshirt looking around nervously. I quickly slipped out of my car and walked around to the back of the bank. I used my Spiderman bracelets to attach a rope web to the top of the building and walk up the side to the roof.

As I was climbing over the ledge, I saw someone standing on the roof looking down the street. I froze not sure what to do. It was a man. He had big strong arms and a lean torso. He definitely resembled Batman as he stood there. He had a tight red shirt with tight black pants that showed off some nicely toned legs. He had a mask on that resembled Batman's and when he turned around and looked at me, I tried not to laugh.

I climbed the rest of the way onto the roof and stood a few feet away from the man. I wasn't sure if he was good or bad, if he was a random civilian trying to be a vigilante or something out of a comic book. If I was going to run into a fictional character on the roof of a bank, why did it have to be a Batman wannabe? Why couldn't I have run into James Bond 2.0? I guess Batman has his sex appeal too if you ignore the fact that he lives in a cave…with bats.

"Who are you and what are you doing here?" I asked the man.

"I'm the Crimson Eagle. Who are you?"

"Koko. What are you doing here?" I asked again.

"I'm looking for crime. You must be the other superhero, who's been taking all the criminals."

"It's not a contest." I said with some attitude.

"Maybe not, but if I have to share my criminals with someone, I'm glad it's a sexy blonde in tight pants."

"If you're a superhero what's your powers?"

"Super strength," he said as he flexed his muscles, "and flying."

I didn't want him to know I was jealous that he could fly, that's one thing I wish I could do, but my brother hadn't found a way, yet.

"What's your power? Finding good shopping deals?" He said with a twinkle in his eye that I wanted to punch out.

Before I could respond, the alarm to the bank went off. Suddenly, I remembered why I was there. We both ran for the ledge. I attached my rope to propel myself down and 'The Crimson Eagle' just jumped off the roof and ran inside the bank. I was half way down the building when I heard Maggie over my walky-talky.

"Koko its Omega Girl. Can you hear me?"

I picked up my walk-talky and said, "Omega Girl, its Koko. What's up?"

"Mark is taking a girl to his room. What do I do?"

"Do you have your phone? Take a video of them going to his room, use your lock picking skills to get the door open, and get the girl out. Tell her if she decides to press charges she isn't the only girl he's done this to, and you have evidence to help convict him."

"Ok, did you catch the robber?"

"I'm trying to do that right now…"

"Oh! I'm sorry. Don't forget to pick me up."

"Mag..Omega girl!"

"Ya, ok, bye."

I put the walky-talky back in my pocket and finished propelling down the side of the building. When I got to the front door, the Crimson Eagle was standing there with a grin on his face.

"It's about time you got here. Did you have to stop and fix your hair?"

"No!" I couldn't think of a better comeback. He was ruining everything. The burglar was tied up with a black eye and a bloody nose, next to the vault. I could hear police sirens in the distance and knew that was my cue to go.

"Did you have to make him bleed?" I asked the Crimson Eagle.

"Yeah, I did. He was a feisty one." With that he gave me a once over, jumped into the air and flew off.

I ran for my car, which I found by pushing the visible/invisible button on my key remote. It took me twenty minutes to get from the bank to Mark's house. As soon as I got there I realized I wasn't going to be able to go into the party, since Maggie was my only way in and she was already inside. I was contemplating hopping the fence again, when I heard Maggie come in over the walky-talky.

"Koko did you remember to pick me up?"

"Yes Omega Girl, I'm outside."

Maggie came out of the party; she told me she stopped Mark, and the girl was going to press charges. Other then my run in with the obnoxious Crimson Eagle, my night was turning out pretty good.

We drove back to the dorms to check in with Leo. When we got back we found him asleep on the floor. We put a blanket over him and went to bed ourselves.

Chapter 7

I'm driving a van. My heart is racing, my palms are sweating and I keep looking for something. I am driving down a six lane road lined with lots of stores and shopping malls. I pull into an alley and sit in the van. After a few seconds a black SUV pulls in on the other side of the alley and drives toward me. The SUV flashes its headlights twice and I get out of my van. I walk toward the SUV and a man with an angry face gets out. He's holding a gun and I almost pee my pants. "I've got what you wanted in the back of the van" I say to the man with the gun. I hear some doors open and five men with guns climb out of the SUV. They walk to the back of my van and I hear the doors to my van open. "We have a deal, right?" I ask the man with the gun. He's looking over my shoulder and nods his head. He looks back at me and says, "right" and then shoots me four times in the chest. I felt each of the bullets slam through my chest and warm blood start dripping down my stomach. I fell backward from the force and the pain was so overwhelming I couldn't keep standing. My legs gave way and I hit my head on the concrete. I heard some yelling and the van and the SUV sped out of the alley.

I opened my eyes and found myself in my dorm room. Leo was snoring on the floor and Maggie looked like she was just waking up.

I rolled over and checked my phone to see what time it was. It was nine in the morning, so I looked at Maggie and asked, "Breakfast?"

"Sounds amazing."

"Should we wake Leo?"

"Yes, we can't leave him here."

I shook Leo until he woke up and then we all walked over to the dining hall to get breakfast. I was really craving eggs and bacon.

When we sat down at our usual table I asked Leo if he found anything useful on Ms. Hayes.

"Unfortunately, I had homework to work on so I only did a background check ,which revealed nothing. But I did hear a rumor in my class the other day that she was sleeping with the art teacher. It might be worth checking into."

"Yeah, that's a good idea. Maybe when you have a chance you could do a background check on the art teacher as well." I told him. "How did things go last night with the party?" I asked Maggie.

"Good. I won a round of beer pong, and I gave my number to this really cute guy who was flirting with me all night."

"Maggie, how did you do stopping Mark on your own?"

"Oh, it was fine I guess. It was kind of scary, and I felt kind of ridiculous. It's a lot easier and more fun to fight crime when you have a friend. I don't want to have to do it alone again."

"That's fair. Hopefully you won't have to."

"How about you? What happened at the bank?" Maggie asked me.

"Well...it went well...the guy got caught...it will probably be on the news...which is cool..."

"Why are you acting weird?" Maggie asked.

"There was a guy there."

"Yeah... we know... a guy robbed the bank." Maggie said.

"No, not that guy. There's another superhero in town and he comes in the form of a disgusting pig in tight pants."

"Is he hot at least?" Leo asked.

Maggie and I both looked over at him with subtle quizzical looks.

"Oh, by the way, I'm gay." Leo said calmly.

"OH MY GOSH! I've always wanted a gay best friend! This is the best news ever! You are no longer just my nerdy friend. You're my nerdy GAY friend!!" Maggie started squealing and jumping up and down in her seat. At one moment she even clapped her hands together.

I was indifferent on the topic, gay or not gay. I just wanted someone who could do good computer searches.

"He was not hot. He looked ridiculous." I said, interrupting Maggie's adoration for Leo.

"What's his super power?" Leo asked.

"He said he had super strength and he can fly."

"Wow, he fly's?" Maggie asked.

"Yes, and he looked stupid doing it!" I said.

"What's his name? Did you get his name?" Leo asked.

"He called himself the Crimson Eagle."

"Oh that's a cool name!" Leo said with excitement.

"Calm down you two. This isn't good for us. He could swoop in and interrupt our crime fighting efforts at any moment."

"Maybe we shouldn't think of it as 'interrupting', but as helping." Maggie said.

"Wait until you meet him, and then tell me if you think he's helpful. It's his fault I didn't catch the robber last night."

"So that's what this is all about. You're mad at him for catching your robber! You hate him, because he might be a better crime fighter than you." Leo said.

"No! That's not it. He's annoying, and made fun of me for being a female crime fighter. That's what this is about, and just so you guys know, I had a vision last night of a guy dying in an alley, so nap between classes, because it's going to be a long night!"

I got up and walked out while Maggie and Leo snickered at me.

I went to my drama class. I was getting frustrated that I hadn't gotten anywhere with finding out who murdered Ms. Hayes. When I walked into the classroom there was an older looking student standing in the front of the class. I took a seat that had a good view of Sky and waited for class to start.

The student in the front introduced herself as an advanced drama student. She told us that she would be running the classroom portion of our class until the school could hire a new teacher. She also wanted to make sure our big school play kept going. She announced that we are going to need a new director and that anyone with experience, who would like to take on the task could let her know. Sky raised his hand and said he had directed a few plays before and would love to direct our school production.

On my way out of class I saw a girl talking to Sky. He looked really into her and the things I was picking up from his mind were turning into a porno. As I walked past, I got jostled in the crowd and someone pushed me. I accidentally fell into the girl talking to Sky and she fell over into one of the lecture hall chairs. When I fell into her I also accidentally elbowed her in the nose which caused her to get a pretty bad nose bleed.

The girl shoved me off of her and said "You bitch! You're going to pay for that!"

I could hear her thoughts and she was thinking about telling her cheer squad about me. I figured there wasn't too much a cheerleader could do. After all I fight criminals every night. I looked over at Sky who was staring down at me and starting to walk away. I tried reading his mind and all he was thinking was "Who is this chick? She looks like my little sister." Great, that's just what every girl wants to hear from the guy she likes.

On my way back to the dorms, I got a phone call from my dad. He called me to see how I was doing and to say that my brother wanted to tell me he was sending me more spy gadgets. I kind of felt like a kid at Christmas; I couldn't wait to see what my brother was sending me.

***

Maggie and I had found the alley I believed was in my vision. We hid my car in a parking lot and I climbed the roof of one of the buildings lining the alley, while Maggie hid behind a dumpster. While we waited for the vans to show up, we entertained ourselves by making funny noises over the walk-talkies.

After two hours I saw the van and SUV coming down the street. Everything was happening just the way I saw it in my vision. Before the SUV showed up Maggie quickly ran around stabbing the van's tires with a knife, so the guys wouldn't be able to drive away with it. When the SUV showed up, I waited for the guys to get out and jumped down on the roof of their car.

The guys that got out of the SUV noticed the slashed tires and then looked up at me. I saw the driver raise his gun at me so I pulled a whip off of my belt and used it to knock the gun out of his hand. Maggie popped out from behind the dumpster and started fighting with some of the guys. A few more guns popped up and I couldn't whip them all. A couple guys started firing at me. I was trying to dodge bullets and keep the guys from killing me. There were men running everywhere and the guy who drove the van realized he had nowhere to go, so he started running down the street. The guy driving the SUV started up his car and the other guys jumped in, as it started driving down the alley. Even though all the guys got away, we came there to prevent a guy from dying and we succeeded. Maggie and I walked over to the van that was still parked in the alley and opened the back. There were boxes from top to bottom, right to left and there was a mixed scent of bad body odor and cardboard. Maggie and I opened one of the boxes and found lots of plastic bags with pills of all different shapes and colors. I closed the van doors and called the police to tell them about it. Maggie and I high-fived and drove back to the dorms.

***

The next day I decided to go to the art teacher's classroom and see what he looked like and maybe read his mind a little. When I found the art classroom there was a woman teaching. The class was just getting out so I asked her if she was the usual art teacher. She informed me that she was stepping in because Mr. Wagner wasn't able to teach for a while, but she didn't know why.

I called Leo and asked him to find out where Mr. Wagner lived, so I could investigate why he wasn't showing up for class. While I walked back to the dorm, I saw a group of people in cheerleading outfits running toward me with baseball bats, hammers, and a few wooden boards. I can fight a lot of people, but there's not much I can do against twenty angry cheerleaders swinging hard objects around. They started yelling and getting closer, so I ran as fast as I could and thought to myself, "it was a good thing they didn't have guns".

The cheerleaders were gaining on me, so I changed directions and headed for the quad. There are always a lot of people in the quad and in these situations it's better to be around a lot of people, who can be eye witnesses to your death. I could hear the girl I knocked over yell, "Get back here bitch!! I'm going to give you a bloody nose!!" I had a feeling she was going to do more than just give me a bloody nose. As I headed into the quad, I almost felt special having the cheerleaders chasing after me. I was no longer invisible. Once I made it out the other side of the quad, the cheerleaders had vanished, so I hurried to the dorms.

Chapter 8

I wandered over to the crime scene in hopes that maybe Ms. Haye's ghost would try to communicate with me, or I could at least find some kind of clue. When I walked into the theater there was caution tape surrounding the stage, but Ms. Hayes's body had been removed. I walked closer to the stage and walked up the steps. I was standing on the stage staring at the place where Ms. Hayes body had been hanging. I didn't see anything on the stage that seemed useful so I looked out into the rows of seats, but everything looked pretty normal there too. I walked between the curtains on the side of the stage looking for something the police might have left behind. While I was looking for some kind of clue on the wood floor, I heard Ms. Hayes voice coming from behind me. I slowly turned around to see Ms. Hayes talking to someone. Actually they were yelling, but the person's back was to me.

The mystery person had gray curly hair and a small frail figure. She was wearing a white blouse, black pencil skirt, and black heals. I was guessing that this person was probably incapable of hanging Ms. Hayes or at least incapable of doing it alone.

I listened in to what they were saying. I walked across the stage to get a better look at the mystery woman's face.

Ms. Hayes was shouting "You are being very unreasonable right now! I am most certainly not sleeping with your son! I was helping him run lines and that is it! How dare you accuse me of something like that!"

The mystery woman was shouting back "Well, we both know it wouldn't be the first time someone has accused you of sleeping with someone you shouldn't be! You also have a thing for people's husband too, don't you slut?!"

The argument was getting pretty heated and was revealing a lot of things I wouldn't have thought Ms. Hayes was capable of, but then again I had only just met the woman. The women were getting more worked up when I accidentally tripped over a box of microphones and the vision went away.

I might have lost the vision before finding out who killed Ms. Hayes, but I wasn't ready to give up investigating that easily. I knew Ms. Hayes had to have an office somewhere. I just wasn't sure where.

I walked to the back of the stage where I was faced with doors. There was one door that led to the hall with all the classrooms, a few more going to all the dressing rooms and another that went outside. I decided to start with the door to the classrooms, because it seemed like the most logical place for an office. I wandered down the hall looking at all the door signs until I finally found one that said 'Ms. Hayes's office'. I ignored the caution tape and tried opening the door. I knew it was kind of a long shot that the door would be unlocked, but I thought it couldn't hurt to try. After the door refused to open I called Maggie to come over and pick the lock.

After twenty minutes of standing outside of Ms. Hayes office and playing on my phone, Maggie showed up and opened the door. Once we were inside we locked the door behind us and started snooping around in Ms. Hayes stuff.

Her office was small with one desk and a few filing cabinets. The cabinets contained tests, scripts and music for the various plays she has directed over the years. She didn't have any photos and her computer was sitting amongst an array of papers on her desk. The office was dimly lit by one light bulb and it smelled like incense and coffee. I rifled through papers while Maggie looked through files and emails on the computer.

After a couple of moments Maggie said, "Did you know the school was cutting the art programs, and subsequently laying off all the art teachers?"

"Ms. Hayes was getting fired?" I asked to clarify.

"According to this email from the dean, all the teachers were getting fired and that includes both Ms. Hayes and Mr. Wagner. Ms.

Hayes sent the president of the university a pretty nasty email back about it too. Her email says she was going to protest and bring attention to the school's budget decision to cut art and fund football. She wrote that if she was going down, she was going to bring everyone down with her. What do you think she meant by that?"

"Well, earlier I had a vision of her fighting with a woman, who was accusing Ms. Hayes of sleeping with the her son and other women's husbands. A few sex scandals and a couple broken marriages would constitute as getting even and as bringing other people down."

"Well, Ms. Hayes had nothing to lose, so it's hard to say what she might have been willing to do."

My phone started dinging to let me know I had a text message. I looked down and saw that Leo had sent me Mr. Wagner's address.

"Leo just texted me Mr. Wagner's number and I didn't find anything useful in the pile of papers on Ms. Hayes desk. Unless you can find anything else on the computer, do you want to go with me to snoop around Wagner's house?"

Maggie clicked on a few more files on the computer and said, "there's nothing else here that's useful. Let's go to Wagner's house."

***

A half hour later we drove up to Mr. Wagner's house dressed in our super hero costumes. We didn't want people to think we were burglars trying to break-in and steal stuff so we wore the costumes. We walked up to the house and went to a side window to see if Mr. Wagner was home.

"Maggie, can you walk around to the other side and see if you see anyone in the house on the other side. I'll check the back." Maggie left and I walked through the side gate. I looked through a sliding glass door into the kitchen. I saw Mr. Wagner stirring something in a pot. The table was set for two and there were candles lit in the middle. Ms. Hayes walked around the corner and gave Mr. Wagner a kiss. Although I couldn't hear what they were saying, they looked happy and in love. I wasn't sure how this vision was helpful, but maybe Ms. Hayes wanted me to see her in a positive light in loo of all the bad things I had discovered earlier in the day. A couple seconds later as Wagner and Hayes sat down to eat the vision faded away.

I heard Maggie walk up next to me and say, "The house is empty and I picked the door lock. You want to go in and look around?"

"Yeah let's go."

We locked the door behind us and split up to cover the house as quickly as possible. We weren't sure if Wagner was going to be coming back soon. I wandered through the living room and looked at pictures he had on his mantel. There was one of a young boy holding up a giant fish, another of an elderly couple, a few more of the same young boy and another boy, and one that looked like a family portrait with the two young boys, a young girl and a couple that looked like their parents. I moved down the hall where I found an office. I looked inside and found painting isles, and sketch boards. The cupboards all had paint and drawing supplies. I was looking for something useful when I heard Maggie shout from upstairs.

"Lennox come check this out!"

I ran up the stairs while yelling, "Where are you?"

"In the bedroom at the end of the hall."

I walked into the bedroom and saw Maggie looking in a drawer by the bed. I looked over her shoulder and saw baggies of pills.

"Do you think Mr. Wagner was doing drugs?" Maggie asked.

"Well, if he wasn't taking them he has enough to sell."

"I also found some bags of white stuff in the closet, that I'm going to guess is cocaine."

"Did you find anything about Ms. Hayes?"

"No, not unless she was doing drugs too."

At that moment the doorbell rang. Maggie and I froze, and looked at each other, neither one of us knowing what to do. We walked down the hall to the room at the end, and looked out the window, to see who was standing at the door.

It was a man who looked annoyed. He was wearing a t-shirt and jeans and had greased back hair and a short pig like nose. He looked around, peering into some of the windows.

"Wait a minute," I said. "That guy looks familiar."

"Oh my gosh! I think that's one of the guys from the alley, that night we found that van full of drug."

"Oh crap! This is bad. We need to get out of here fast, and run for the car."

The man had walked to the back of the house where we could hear him yelling, "I know you're in there Wagner! The boss wants his money! If you don't come out, then I'm coming in!"

Maggie and I ran down the stairs and bolted for the front door. The man saw us from the back door and started yelling at us. We were half way down the drive way when we heard a gunshot coming from behind us.

"Crap, he's shooting at us! Just keep running!" I yelled to Maggie who was looking behind her at the man.

The man was yelling "You bitches better get back here! You cost my boss thousands of dollars! You bitches are going to pay for that!"

He fired off a few more rounds in our direction as I pushed a button on my key remote to turn my car on, before we got to it. We flung the car doors open and leaped inside. As soon as we shut the doors I locked them.

Maggie shouted, "What are you doing! Stop wasting time, he's getting closer!" Maggie ducked down as the man shot off a few more shots.

"I'm trying to get the key in the ignition! The car's bullet proof, we'll be fine!"

"Oh, great! I feel so much better now that I know your car is bullet proof!" Maggie said sarcastically.

I was finally able to drive off as the guy shouted, "I'll find you!"

***

The next night Maggie, Leo and I were sitting in our dorm room. We were just talking about random things when Maggie looked at me and said, "Lennox, how did you get your ability to read minds and have visions?"

"Well, I can't say for sure, but I think it all started when I was a kid and I got struck by lightning."

"You got hit by lighting? That's crazy! You survived lightning? Wow!" Leo said.

Maggie was sitting on her bed reading a magazine and wearing sweats. She said, "Why do you think you got your powers from getting hit by lighting?"

"Well, I didn't have any of the powers, until after it happened and the doctors had to resuscitate me back to life. I read somewhere that near death experiences can connect you to the dead."

"I wish something cool like that could have happened to me. Do you have any marks from the lightning?" Leo asked

"Yeah, I do. I've never shown anyone, but I guess I could show you guys." I pulled my shirt down to reveal my left shoulder.

There was a red mark going down my shoulder toward the middle of my back. It resembled a lightning bolt, but not the cartoon drawn kind. Like a real lightning bolt, with little lines coming from a main line. Like a bunch of nerves.

Leo got up and looked at it closer, "Wow, that is the coolest thing I've ever seen!"

Maggie came over and looked and said "I can't decide if I'm creeped out or impressed!"

"Alright, enough about me. Can you guys help me fight crime tonight?"

"My sorority said I needed to stay in my dorm room tonight, I'm not allowed to go anywhere, but they didn't say why."

"Ok, well that's a little weird, but what about you Leo?"

"I would like to help you, but I have a big paper due tomorrow that I really need to focus all my attention on."

Leo leaves to go back to his dorm to work on his paper, and I start talking to Maggie about Ms. Hayes' murder.

"So we have learned that Mr. Wagner is doing drugs, but we don't know if Ms. Hayes was and we know Ms. Hayes was getting fired, and that she was possibly sleeping around with people and maybe students."

"Well, we don't know she was sleeping with a student. We just know she was maybe sleeping with someone's son." I corrected Maggie.

"Right, and we know she was fighting with someone, who was accusing her of infidelity on the very stage that she was murdered, but you don't think the woman killed her?"

"Correct, so we have collected a good amount of evidence and several places to look further for suspects."

"Where's the next place we are going to look?"

"Her house. There should be clues at her house. I think we should also check out the football coach, since she was mad at the school for continuing to fund football."

"Sounds good to me!"

Maggie's phone started playing a song to indicate she has a phone call. She talked for a few minutes and then announced that the sorority called and told her to go down stairs. I've never been interested in joining a sorority, but I was a little curious about what they do. I decided to follow her down the stairs. We are on the third floor, but once you are in the stair well there is a window looking out onto the parking lot on every level. I waited at the top, until I saw Maggie walk out the door, and then I ran down the stairs and waited by the window at the bottom.

I watched Maggie walk over to a group of young, cold, and kind of scared looking girls standing on the side walk, by the parking lot. After a couple of seconds, three cars pulled up next to them. About six girls wearing Greek letters got out holding bandanas. I could hear one girl saying, "We promise that you will have fun tonight, and what lies ahead will be exciting and special. It's more fun if you are blind folded and surprised by where we are taking you. However, if you are not comfortable being blind folded you don't have to be. Raise your hand if you don't want us to blind fold you." The girls standing on the side walk nervously looked at each other, but nobody raised their hands. "Good, then let's get going."

All the girls on the side walk were blind folded and carefully placed into cars. Then the three cars proceeded to drive around the parking lot a couple of times weaving in between cars, before driving out and heading toward the sorority houses. I ran into the parking lot to get into my car, so I could follow them. When I got to the spot where I had parked my car, there was a car that I was pretty sure was mine completely covered in saran wrap and had the word BITCH written across the back window. I was staring at my car, trying to figure out if it was worth still trying to follow Maggie or not, when my phone started ringing.

Leo was calling me to tell me there was a fire in a nearby neighborhood.

"I thought you had a paper to write? What are you doing listening to the police scanner?"

"I can do both. I know you wanted to fight crime, so I turned the scanner on, in case anything good came across it. I've also got my walky-talky on, so I can stay in-touch with you."

"Awesome, thanks Leo! Text me the address!"

I started tearing at the saran wrap with full force, and then I ran upstairs to grab everything I would need. Then I got back into my car and drove off to the fire. When I pulled up to the apartment complex that was on fire, I noticed that the street was lined with ambulances, fire trucks, and police cars. I stayed near the bushes along the sidewalk and hid behind fire trucks, while I tried to get a good view of the building. Fire fighters were pulling people out as fast as they could, but the fire had spread across four apartments and was starting to take over a fifth. I saw my mom bossing around a couple of police officers in the middle of the street as they tried keeping by-standers away. I was looking for a way into the building, when I nearly jumped a foot in the air at the sound of a deep voice behind me.

"What are you doing?"

I looked around and saw the Crimson Eagle standing over me.

"You scared me! I'm hiding. Would you get down?"

"Exciting! What are we hiding from?" He whispered as he crouched down behind a big green bush with me.

"None of your business, don't you have something better to do?"

"Yeah! I guess I could probably go save someone, but the news crew hasn't shown up yet."

"So you're going to let people die, because the press hasn't arrived yet?"

"Well, I don't think anyone is dying yet. The firefighters look like they have it mostly under control."

"Well, I for one don't need media attention to commit a heroic act, and if I can get the people out, then the firefighters can focus on fighting the fire."

"Why don't you just go for it then? Why are you hiding in the bushes?"

"I'm waiting for the perfect moment."

"You're scared!"

"I am not!"

"Then go for it, right now!"

"Ok, fine. I'm a little scared of fire. It's hot, and loud, and could kill me."

"Hahahaha, the super hero is scared of fire?"

"Oh, and you don't have any fears?"

"No, because I'm a real super hero."

I was spitting out my response, when he took off, by jumping into the air, and flying toward the building. He disappeared inside the burning building. I didn't want him to get all the credit, so I walked out from behind the bushes. Standing near the edge of the building, I shot a web rope up to the top of the building. I proceeded to climb the wall and crawl into a window that had been blown out by the fire. It was really smoky and I could hardly see anything. I didn't hear anyone yelling for help, so I was hoping everyone had made it out ok. I carefully walked into one of the rooms on the other side of the burnt out wall and saw the Crimson Eagle lying on the ground next to a little toddler who was crawling under a burnt bed. I scooped up the toddler and shielded his tiny body with mine as a piece of the roof fell down. I started shaking the Crimson Eagle.

"Crimson Eagle, wake up! Are you ok? Wake up!"

He wasn't moving and the building was getting more unstable by the second. The fire fighters were spraying water on one part of the building, and I could hear them hammering away at the roof. I ran for the closest window, and shot a web to the roof. While holding the baby I propelled down where I was met by a firefighter and a frantic mother.

The mother grabbed her baby and between sobs sputtered, "Thank you...sniff sniff...thank you!"

I shot back up to the window by retracting the web, a process I don't use often because sometimes the rope gets stuck when it retracts that quickly. I climbed through the window and found that the Crimson Eagle was awake, but trapped behind a burning piece of fallen ceiling.

"Hey girl! Can you get this wood moved?"

"Maybe. If you call me by my name."

"I don't remember your name. I'm...cough cough...getting smoke inhalation. Just help me get out of here."

I wanted to argue, but I also didn't want to stay in the building any longer. I looked around and found a small wooden chair. I used the chair to push the burning piece of wood away enough for him to get out. He stumbled toward me and I said, "We are going to have to go down the stairs, because you can't fly and I can't carry you down with my ropes."

We carefully walked toward the stairs. The Crimson Eagle was leaning on me, and I was trying to see where I was going through the smoke, flames, and my mask. It was a long, scary and treacherous walk down the wobbly staircase. We had to dodge some falling fire and every time we paused to catch our footing, the Crimson Eagle got a little heavier on my shoulders.

After what felt like a long time, we finally made it out the front door. Both of us collapsed on the ground gasping for air. Some firefighters rushed over to assist us. They tried putting an oxygen mask on the Crimson Eagle, while not removing his mask. Once I caught my breath, I told them I would take him to the hospital myself. I didn't want to risk exposing his identity. The guy might be obnoxious, but I hoped he would do the same for me.

The firefighters let me take the Crimson Eagle, and as we walked off, I saw my mom walking toward me. I kept walking as if I hadn't seen her. The last thing I wanted at that moment was to get into a fight with my mom. I was trying to get the Crimson Eagle into my car, while the police tried to keep the photographers at bay, as ordered by my mother. My mom came up behind me and said, "You could have died in there. I wish you wouldn't do that!"

"Well, you don't always get what you wish for."

I got into my car, turned it invisible and sped off toward the hospital. By the time I was a couple blocks away, the Crimson Eagle was acting like himself again.

He said, "Good thing you were there tonight, otherwise I would have had to take all the credit for saving that baby."

"You didn't save the baby! I did, and if I hadn't been there tonight, you probably would have died in the fire."

"Nah, I would have found a way out."

My walky-talky went off, Leo said, "Hey, Koko! Are you ok? I haven't heard from you for a while."

The Crimson Eagle couldn't hear Leo since I had the ear piece in, so at the same time he said, "Drop me off here. I'll get myself to the hospital."

As I pulled over to the side of the road I picked up the walky-talky and said, "Blue Sleuth I'm fine. I'll be home in a few minutes."

The Crimson Eagle asked, "Who are you talking to? Are there more people like us?"

"I don't work alone." Was all I said.

The Crimson Eagle shut the car door, and I drove back to the dorms.

Chapter 9

After Maggie and I came back from breakfast, we sat in our room. I was trying to get Maggie to say what happened with the sorority, but she wasn't budging. We heard a knock at our door. Maggie went and answered it. She opened the door to find Leo standing there holding up the morning paper. Maggie grabbed it and looked at the cover, while Leo came inside.

Leo looked at me and said, "It's official! Your famous."

"Oh my gosh!" Maggie squealed as she shut the door. "I can't believe this! The one time I'm not with you, and you get photographed!"

"There have been a lot of times you weren't with me, and it's not the first time that I've been photographed. It's just the first time in California."

"Well this Crimson Eagle guy looks kind of hot."

"How can you tell? You can't even see his face." I said

"Oh you can tell. He's got tight pants that show a nice butt, a shirt to reveal strong arms and a six pack." Leo said while he looked over Maggie's shoulder.

***

I went to the drama building, to work on painting some sets for the play. I was painting outside, because the students were having rehearsal inside on the stage. Occasionally, when someone opened the door, I could hear Sky barking out directions to people on stage. This was the first time they had been able to use the stage, since the police took down the caution tape.

People were running all over the place, talking and laughing. I didn't think anyone would notice if I slipped off. I thought this would be a good opportunity to talk to people about Ms. Hayes murder, and explore around for clues. Getting to see Sky direct was just a nice bonus to the plan.

I walked through the door, as if I was going inside to get something. I saw Sky wearing a black t-shirt and jeans, holding a clip board, and wearing a headset. He was standing on stage showing someone how to deliver their line. He looked very handsome and important, while he told everyone what to do.

I wandered back stage to where the dressing rooms were located. There were lots of people coming in and out of the rooms. I felt like I was getting in the way and other then costumes and make-up, there wasn't much to see. I wandered over to the side of the stage, just as Sky was walking off. I held my breath, as he walked past me. He smelled of sweet cologne and laundry detergent. He wore a long sleeved grey shirt with our school logo on it. He didn't notice me, as he walked to the front of the stage.

I turned around and walked down the hall of classrooms over to Ms. Hayes's office. As I walked by, I looked through the window and saw Ms. Hayes passionately kissing a very young looking man. I stopped to watch, knowing this was a vision that Ms. Hayes was sending me for some reason. The guy had on a sweatshirt with our school name on it, but as soon as I noticed it, he ripped it off. His brown hair could have benefited from a haircut, but his strong facial features made up for it. Ms. Hayes was sitting on her desk and pulling her skirt up. The guy was unbuttoning her blouse while kissing her neck. I heard Ms. Hayes say to him, "quick Ryan, before someone walks by. I can't explain to the janitor a second time that I was helping you with your costume." Ryan started unzipping his pants and the vision disappeared.

I heard a noise to my right and I looked over to see the janitor mopping the floors. He looked at me and said, "It's a tragedy she died. She had some questionable behavior, but she treated me like I was somebody, and I'll never forget that."

"Did you talk to her a lot?" I asked him, trying to pry information out of him without raising suspicion.

"Oh I guess. She would be here late at night sometime. Just a writin' things and sometimes a talkin' on the phone. You know the night she died, I seen her talkin' on the phone goin' on about black mail. She was sayin' she had some and she wasn't afraid tu use it."

"How strange. I wonder what it could have been?"

"I don't know. She had lots a students in her office and I don't think she was a helpin' them with their costumes."

"Sounds like you could have had some blackmail on her."

"I guess su, but I never saw her doin' anythin' bad. I wouldn't a done nothin' to her either, she was a nice lady."

"If you were hear the night she died, did you see who killed her?"

"No, if I had I would've pounded him in tu the ground. But after this old lady talked tu 'er there was a girl her' in a cheerleadin' outfit."

"Could you describe this girl?"

"Uh, she 'as tall, blonde, perty with a real angry face."

"Interesting. It was nice meeting you. Have a nice day!" I said with a smile and a wave.

"Oh yeah. You, tu!" He said with a big grin that was missing a few teeth.

The janitor had proven to be very helpful and the list of suspects was getting longer and longer. The last person to see her alive was now a cheerleader. I had a feeling it was the same cheerleader that was out to get me. She seemed to have some anger management issues. I don't think she has what it would have taken to hang Ms. Hayes, but maybe if she had the whole squad helping her? Still, it was hard to see the cheerleaders committing murder, but then the whole squad had no problem chasing me through campus with baseball bats and hammers.

I headed back to the dorms and found Leo. I told Leo what I had learned that afternoon and he told me he read a notice online that Ms. Hayes will be buried tomorrow. If I wanted to see her body before she was buried, I needed to get to the morgue as soon as possible. I still needed to look at her house, and snoop around the football locker rooms. I'm sure Maggie would want to join me for the last one.

Once Maggie got back from class, we decided to go to dinner together. Leo had a late class that night, so he had eaten dinner earlier. We talked about classes and boys, while we ate slices of pizza and side salad.

On our way out of the dining hall I spotted a cheerleader uniform through the glass door. I grabbed Maggie's arm to stop her from walking and said, "Do you see the cheer outfits? We might have to make a run for it."

"How did they find us?"

"Well, it's not like we're hard to find. If we aren't in classes, we are probably going to be at the dorms, or in the dining hall."

We walked toward the door keeping an eye out for more cheerleaders. I spotted another one to the far left watching people walk past. As we walked through the door, I saw two more standing along the path to the dorms.

"Maggie they are blocking us from the dorms, let's run for my car."

"Ok! Run fast!"

I started running for my car as a cheerleader came out of nowhere and we narrowly dodged a swing of a toilet plunger. I felt something hit my back and looked behind me to see a cheerleader throwing eggs at us. Another cheerleader nailed Maggie in the head with a coke bottle.

"Ow! What did I ever do to them?"

"Be friends with me?" I guessed.

We took a sharp turn at the parking lot and tried hiding between cars as we worked our way to where mine was parked. I was pretty sure we had lost them, so we ran for my car. When we found my poor car, it was covered with window paint. There was "Bitch" written across the back window, "Slut", "Cunt", and "Ugly" written across the side windows and "Whore" written across the windshield. There were some nice little decorations of skull and bones, and penis's.

We got in and started driving off when two SUV's pulled up behind us. Each car had six to eight cheerleaders hanging out from windows chucking eggs and what appeared to be water balloons filled with water and syrup. There was a syrup streak dripping down the word "Cunt". I was trying to drive through traffic only able to see through the bottom of the 'H' in "Whore". I took a left out of the parking lot, and sped through the yellow light, hoping the cheerleaders would get stuck behind a red light, but they stayed on my tail and made it through.

Maggie shouted, "Put the car in invisible mode so they can't see us!"

"I can't, because they will get suspicious about my car, and might guess that I'm Koko. We are just going to have to ditch them the old fashioned way."

The cheerleaders were getting aggressive with the throwing and were yelling obscenities at us. I ignored a stop sign, while looking around for cops. We sped through a few more traffic lights and ended up on Washington St., the busiest street in town. I was dodging cars in the far right two lanes and the cheerleaders were driving along side of us in the far left lane. As they threw things at us, they would occasionally hit an innocent car instead of mine, which was sparking some road rage. Now I had cheerleaders and random citizens mad at me.

I took a sudden right handed turn and the cheerleaders couldn't get over in time. I took that opportunity to get turned around and drive back toward the dorms, but this time taking all the back streets, so they wouldn't be able to spot me. We were about half way back when I got a call on my phone.

"Maggie, I can't grab my phone, while I'm driving, can you reach into my pocket and pull it out."

"Sure, which pocket is it in?"

"My front right pocket."

I tried straightening my leg without pushing the gas pedal harder, so it would be easier for Maggie to get my phone. She wiggled it out and answered. After a few seconds she hung up and said, "Leo says there was a break-in at the art teacher's house, and the police are there now."

I pushed my cars GPS on and said, "Mr. Wagner's house." The GPS calculated our directions and we changed course again. As we got closer to Mr. Wagner's street I parked around the corner, and away from the police cars. Maggie and I got out and quietly crouched closer to the scene, while hiding alongside someone's house. I was watching what was going on, and looking around for my mom. I was thankful I could change into my crime fighting outfit, since I didn't have a quick way to get egg out of fabric. Maggie was pulling glass out of her hair, and redoing her ponytail, when I heard someone laughing and walking up behind us. I had a sinking feeling I knew who it was, and I wasn't excited about it.

The person said, "So who did you piss off, to get the nice car decorations?"

Maggie turned around and said, "Oh, my gosh! It's the Crimson Eagle!" Her eyes were big and she was practically drooling.

"It's another hot crime fighting chick?!" the Crimson Eagle said while looking at Maggie. "Nice to meet you. I'm the Crimson Eagle." He said, while kissing Maggie's hand.

Maggie was practically fainting as she sputtered, "I'm mmaaa mm…ummm..lllaaa…Omega girl."

"Omega girl, focus. The police are saying that they don't know if anything is missing in the house, as far as they can tell, and that they are still looking for Wagner. He's their primary suspect in Ms. Hayes murder, because he's been missing. They think he's hiding from them."

"Are you guys trying to solve that murder at the college?" The Crimson Eagle asked.

"Maybe." I said.

"Well, I have an inside connection to the police department. I could help you."

"That would be great!" Maggie said with a smile.

"We will think about it." I said glaring at Maggie.

Maggie saw my glare and responded with a silent, "What?"

The police were starting to leave so the three of us crawled closer to the house. Once the police had left, we walked over to the house. Maggie picked the lock and we went inside. The house was completely torn apart top to bottom. There was over turned furniture, knocked over shelves, broken picture frames and dishes, food scattered everywhere, and drawers pulled out and turned over. It was hard walking anywhere, without stepping on anything.

"Omega girl, quick, lets run upstairs and see if the drugs are still there. I didn't hear the police say anything about finding drugs."

"They wouldn't have been able to take the drugs anyway without a search warrant." The Crimson Eagle said.

The three of us climbed over furniture and ran for the stairs. We raced up the stairs Maggie first, followed by me and the Crimson Eagle behind. As we got to the top of the stairs the Crimson Eagle said to me, "You have a cute butt."

I turned around and gave him a mad face that was lost under my mask. Maggie turned around and said, "Stop flirting you two."

I threw my left elbow backward as hard as I could, nailing him right in the middle of the chest, before we got through the bedroom door. The Crimson Eagle stopped to grab his chest, and catch his breath. We didn't have to look very hard, since all the drawers were pulled out, and it was very obvious, any drugs that had been in this house were long gone.

"Since the drugs appear to be the only things missing, we can probably assume it was the drug dealers." I said.

"Well, if it was the drug dealers, I for one, would like to get out of here, before they show up, and start shooting at us again." Maggie said.

"You girls just really know how to make friends, don't you?" The Crimson Eagle said.

"Shut up." I said.

The Crimson Eagle smiled, and then said more seriously, "Well, the police had a theory the drug dealers killed Ms. Hayes, out of retaliation."

"Oh, crap, that reminds me. We need to get to the morgue tonight." I said.

"Oh great! That's exactly how I was hoping to spend my Friday night." Maggie said sarcastically.

"I'll go with you girls. You might need someone there, in case you get scared." The Crimson Eagle said.

"We don't need your help." I said to him.

"Well, actually, I don't think it would hurt to have a third person with us. Then I don't actually have to go into the morgue. I can just be a look out." Maggie said, while leaving to search the rest of the house.

I thought for a moment, and then answered, "Ok, fine." I looked at the Crimson Eagle and said, "But if we are going to let you come along, you have to share everything you know about the drama teacher's murder."

"Deal," he said while putting his hand out for me to shake. I could see a little twinkle in his eye, and I was a little hesitant to shake his hand, but I did it anyway. As soon as he grabbed my hand, he yanked me toward him. My heart skipped a little beat, as we made eye contact. He whispered to me, "I always wanted to go on a date to the morgue."

I tried taking a step back. With some attitude I said, "It's not a date." He matched my step back, with a step forward, and pinned me against a wall. While maintaining eye contact and still holding my hand, he pressed his body closer, and lowered his mouth toward mine. I was super tense and part of me wanted to knee him in the nuts, and another part of me was dying to know what his lips tasted like. He was a half centimeter away from my lips, I could feel his breath and smell his shampoo, when Maggie said, "Well, I checked the bathroom and his sleeping pills, allergy medicine and inhaler are all there, but he's missing toilet paper."

I pushed the Crimson Eagle away from me and said, "Ok, let's go." I hurriedly ran down the stairs. We all piled into the car and took off toward the morgue. On the drive over there, we exchanged information. The only new information the Crimson Eagle contributed was the police had recovered a computer and journal from Ms. Hayes house and it documented everyone she had been sleeping with. It also detailed Ms. Hayes desperate attempts to get pregnant with In Vitro fertilization.

"Do you know the names of everyone she slept with?" I asked him.

"No." He said, "She used code words, not names to refer to all the people. The journal said she had evidence she was going to use for blackmail, but the police searched her whole house and haven't been able to find any evidence."

"Tomorrow, let's go to her house." I said.

Maggie turned around to look at the Crimson Eagle in the backseat. "Can I get your number, so we can call you tomorrow?"

"I don't have a cell phone, I'm a super hero who works alone."

"Well, don't you have a phone you use, when you aren't being a super hero?" Maggie said.

"Yes, but I can't give you that number. It could compromise my secret identity."

"That's a good point. Maybe we should have separate phones for crime fighting?" Maggie asked me.

"We don't need to, because when we are crime fighting, we use the walky-talky's, but I have a pay-as-you-go cell phone in my trunk, I can give you." I said very matter-of-factly to the Crimson Eagle. "That way we can get a hold of you if there's some old lady who needs help crossing the street."

I was about to put my car in invisible mode, when I remembered it was still covered in food. I thought we should run through a car wash before arriving at our destination.

"Alright team, let's go! It looks like the morgue is closed, but there might be people around, so we need to be quiet. Omega girl, make sure your walky-talky is on."

I said into the walky-talky, "Blue Sleuth, we are at the morgue. Do you copy?"

Leo's voice came over the walky-talky and said, "I'm not sure what you're asking, but I'm here. Let me know when you leave, so I know you got out safely."

"Over and out!" Maggie piped in.

I gave her a look that said, "You're a dork."

The Crimson Eagle was already walking up to the building. We came up behind him. He said, "Looks like all the windows are shut so we can't fly in."

"Omega girl, after you." I said motioning toward the morgue entrance.

Maggie took a few seconds, to pick the lock on the door, and we walked in. As soon as we got in I got goose bumps and realized we didn't know where we were going.

"Where do they keep the bodies?" Maggie whispered.

"I'm not sure. Check all the rooms." I said. The first room the Crimson Eagle opened was the reception area. The room on the other side looked like an office of some kind. We walked down the hall, which had a low ceiling and exposed pipes. At the end, we found a big empty room with chairs. Further down the hall were two big doors. "I bet the bodies are in there!"

I walked to the two doors and pushed one open. Maggie stayed in the hall, while the Crimson Eagle followed me inside. The room had tile floors, and rows of metal doors. There were metal counters and a couple long cabinets. The room had a very distinct smell of something truly awful mixed with cleaning product. I was trying not to throw-up, as I looked at the Crimson Eagle, who was already pulling out bodies from the metal doors.

"How are you so comfortable with this?"

"I took an anatomy class, once. You get used to the smell and you stop thinking of the bodies as real people."

"Yeah, ok. I'm going to see if I can find her file in these filing cabinets."

Fortunately, everything was alphabetized, so it was easy to find. I read through the file which said that Ms. Hayes was killed by a blunt force object, not asphyxiation. That meant whoever killed her, had to be strong enough to hit her, and then hang her up. That also meant there was a murder weapon, and either the police already had it, or it's still out in the world somewhere. The file also listed the sexually transmitted diseases Ms. Hayes had, and it didn't say anything about her being pregnant. There was nothing else in the file that seemed helpful so I put it back in the cabinet and looked around for the Crimson Eagle.

"Did you find her body yet?" I swallowing a little vomit, while he zipped open a body bag.

"Not yet. You could help me look."

"Yeah, I could." I said, but didn't move.

Maggie stuck her head in and whispered loudly, "Would you two hurry up. I'm getting nervous out here."

"We're working on it!" I loudly whispered back at her.

"Oh, we're working on it?" The Crimson Eagle said.

"Shut up." I said back.

It only took a couple more body bags, before the Crimson Eagle finally found Ms. Hayes. As he zipped her bag open I walked over while holding my nose shut. She looked calm and peaceful. You could see a mark on her head, where she got hit, and she had marks around her neck from the rope. There wasn't much else to see on the corpse, but I made note of the way the head injury looked. We zipped the bag up and slid her back into the hole in the wall.

We walked out the door, and almost collided with Maggie who whispered, "Someone's coming!"

Maggie pulled us toward a side door. We slipped in as a shadow approached around the corner. The room we walked into was small with metal tables and cabinets. There was one window in the back that we ran for. Maggie started trying to get the window open, but it wouldn't budge. The Crimson Eagle pushed us aside to open it. After a few tugs, he got the window open and we all climbed out. We ran for the car, and right before we got there, the

Crimson Eagle yelled "Bye ladies." He jumped into the air, and flew away.

Chapter 10

The next day Maggie and I went to Ms. Hayes' house. She lived in a quiet neighborhood in the middle of town. The houses were generally all one story. Most of the lawns were a bit overgrown and brown. The houses were cute in a 'grandma's house' kind of way and the cars in the drive-ways were probably as old as your grandma. We approached the house, while looking around to make sure nobody was watching us. Maggie tried the door knob, and when it didn't open, she picked the lock. We walked in to find a small house, with wooden floors and multi-colored walls. There were lots of paintings and artifacts decorating the walls and the mantel piece. There was a strong smell of incense and cat litter. Maggie wandered down the hall, and I examined the pictures sitting above the small brick fireplace. There were pictures with people, who looked like family members, and one that had about ten kids of various ages. I was guessing they were her cousins. I suddenly heard yelling coming from behind me. I quickly turned around, while whipping my fists into the air ready to fight. I saw Ms. Hayes standing in the doorway, yelling at the drug dealers.

Ms. Hayes said, "I have no idea where he is, I can't help you."

"We are going to find him Lady. If you've been hiding him, it's not going to end well for you!" The drug dealer said.

"I understand that, but I've been teaching all day. I don't know where he is." Ms. Hayes said right before the drug dealer reached forward and grasped his hand around her neck.

"Your boyfriend is dead meat, and I would love to serve you as a side dish. You better hope we don't find you with him." The drug dealer said with a snarl. He turned around and walked down the drive-way. Ms. Hayes shut the door and locked it. She quickly turned around, almost walking right into me. I fell over onto the couch, trying to get out of the way. I watched her walk into the kitchen. There was a mask from one of those African tribes on the wall, staring at me, so I moved into the kitchen.

There were herb plants on the window sill and pictures of chickens and vegetables on red colored walls. Ms. Hayes was warming up a tea kettle. She walked to a door next to the cabinets. When she opened the door, Mr. Wagner walked into the kitchen, from what appeared to be the garage.

Ms. Hayes said to him, "I can't keep covering up for you. I've loaned you money for your drug habit, but, I can't do it again. You need to find a way to pay them off. Until you do, you can't come over here anymore."

Mr. Wagner sighed and rubbed his face with his hand. "I know, I just don't know where to get the money, and I'm running out of places to hide. I only have five of the ten pounds of drugs they gave me to sell. I sold five pounds to college students, but they wouldn't pay full price. I sold the drugs to them at half price. I thought I could sell the other five pounds at twice the price to my adult clients, but I haven't found any clients, who are willing to pay twice the normal price."

"It doesn't seem like it was smart to sell drugs at half price." Ms. Hayes said while pouring a cup of tea.

"I had to sell something to someone and fast, or they were going to kill me."

"Why would they kill you, if you just handed the drugs back?"

"Because I know who they are, where they get their drugs and who their clients are. It would be a liability for them to just let me walk. They might think I was an undercover cop and kill me anyway. They are drug dealers, killing people is just what they do!"

With that comment the two of them disappeared. I was left alone in the kitchen. I turned around to face the dining hall and saw Ms. Hayes again, sitting at the table and talking on the phone.

"Mr. Coleman, I don't care how much money got cut from the budget, it's a travesty to get rid of the arts!" Ms. Hayes said. "No, I will not leave this alone. You cannot give $50,000 to the football program for Freshman recruits next year, when the drama department has no money for costumes!" There was a pause as Mr. Coleman spoke on the other end. "It doesn't matter how I know about the football program. What's important is that you are favoring them." Pause. "I understand the football brings in more money than theater productions, but theater makes more money than Math, Science, Law, Economics..." Pause. "How dare you say that! Art programs are just as important as every other major! We need actors to make movies, to bring in revenue for Holllywood, and Los Angeles, and in turn for the state of California, and foreign movie sales bring revenue to the United States, so the theater program helps the United States of America!" Pause. "I am not leaping! Someone designed that coffee mug on your desk, the painting you have in your living room, and the vase you bought to put your wife's flowers in. Those things wouldn't be here, for your pleasure, if it wasn't for the art programs! There are kids who are terrible at Math, but find joy in pottery making and that kid shouldn't be excluded from college, because you decided to cut the art programs!" Pause. "I might not have anything really good on you yet, but I've hired someone to dig up dirt on you so you better watch your back Mr. Coleman. If you're going to take me down, I'm going to take you down with me!"

With that final sentence, she hung up the phone. I went to find Maggie down the hall. I found her in the bedroom sitting in front of a small bookcase. She was flipping through a yearbook.

"Hey Lennox, look at this. It's an old yearbook from 1995 at Kennedy High School and it lists Ronald Clark our football coach as a senior, but Ms. Hayes isn't in it. Then she has this other yearbook for 1995 at Emerson Junior High and it shows her as an eighth grader. The Junior High year book has signatures from people addressing Ms. Hayes and saying that they thought she did great in the school musical. The high school year book has no signatures in it, but lots of hearts around every picture of Mr. Clark. What do you think this means?"

"My best guess is that she had a crush on Mr. Clark and bought his high school yearbook, but she was only in Junior High at the time."

"She must have really liked him to go to all the effort of buying a year book from a different school, only to put hearts around some of the pictures." Maggie said.

"Was there anything else interesting in here, besides the yearbooks?" I asked her.

"No, you can tell the police have already been through here."

Maggie put the yearbook back and got up. "But I haven't checked the bathroom yet." She walked out of the bedroom and across the hall into the bathroom.

I stood in the bedroom, looking under the bed, just in case Maggie missed something. While I was staring at a giant dust bunny, I heard the bed start to squeak and some moans come from above my head. I was scared to look, but I knew I was having this vision for a reason and I needed to see why. I tentatively lifted my head just enough to see over the edge of the bed and I found myself at eye level with a thick hairy thigh and a very white hairless calf. The moans were getting lauder and turning into faint screams. I moved my eyes toward the top of the bed and saw Mr. Clark lying on his back and Ms. Hayes riding him like a cowgirl. That was all I needed to see, so I quickly ducked down next to the bed. Even though I knew they couldn't see me, I felt the need to crawl out of the bedroom.

When I got into the hallway, I was met by black yoga pants. I looked up to see Maggie with her arms crossed staring down at me.

"What the hell are you doing?" Maggie asked.

"I saw Ms. Hayes having sex with Mr. Clark, and I didn't want to disturb them."

"How considerate of you?" Maggie said with confusion.

I stood up and said, "Did you find anything in the bathroom, or in that extra room across the hall?"

"No, the extra room is completely dedicated to her cat. The bathroom had nothing but nice smelling soap and feminine products."

"Alright, I guess we can go then."

***

Twenty minutes later we walked into our dorm room. We were working on homework, when Leo walked in. We filled him in on what we found at Ms. Hayes house and he said he would ask his roommate when would be the best time to see the coach. We also discussed impersonating reporters. We would be doing a story on Ms. Hayes for a school blog. That might keep him from wondering why we are asking so many questions. We decided that we would tell him an unnamed source told us about the relationship between him and Ms. Hayes.

The next day when Leo found Maggie and me in the dining hall, he told us that the football players had practice at four that afternoon and we should go before that to talk to the coach. The three of us walked over to the football stadium across the street from campus. We headed for the locker rooms, and to the coach's offices.

We found Mr. Clark sitting at his desk in his office at the back of the locker room. There were a few guys getting ready for practice, but the locker room wasn't full yet. The coach looked startled to see us, but he was friendly and eager to answer questions, for a school blog.

Maggie walked in, and shook his hand. "Hi! My name is Maggie and Lennox and I were hoping you could tell us about your relationship with Ms. Hayes. We won't include it in the final written article, but we are trying to figure out as much as we can about Ms. Hayes. We want to write a well rounded story on her. We want to know as much as possible about her personal and professional life as possible."

The coach looked around at the three of us and said, "Who told you I had a relationship with Ms. Hayes?"

Maggie piped up first, "It's an unnamed source. We can't tell you. The interesting thing is you were having a relationship with her and now she's dead. Did you do it?"

"No! I was sleeping with her, but I didn't want my wife to find out. She was kind of annoying, and talked a lot, but she was…you know…sexy." He said. "I don't know what I can tell you. We didn't talk much. If you know what I mean?"

Maggie asked, "Well you could help by telling us how you two met, why sleeping with her was worth the risk of getting caught, and about any conversations you had."

I noticed he had a picture frame on his desk. It was him, a woman, a young boy and a teenage girl. I recognized the woman as the one I saw yelling at Ms. Hayes the night she died. That means Ms. Hayes was sleeping with Mr. Clark's son.

Mr. Clark had started answering Maggie's questions. "We met last year, when I went to one of the drama club's plays. My daughter wanted to go, because she really likes musicals. I slept with her, because she offered. When my son got caught spray painting a penis going into a butt hole, on the wall of the drama department, I negotiated with Ms. Hayes to let him join the drama club, in exchange for not getting suspended from football. Now he likes drama so much, I'm worried he's going to throw away his football career for Shakespeare. I wasn't worried about getting caught. My wife thinks I spend all my time here in the office, working on coaching."

We thanked Mr. Clark, and started walking out of the locker room. Before we made it out someone, yelled Leo's name. We all turned around to see a tall slender guy with a six pack, and football pants, hopping over benches and coming toward us.

Leo said, "Hi Max."

Max came over and introduced himself to us. Leo said, "This is Max. We have a class together."

"I was hoping you would like to study with me for our test?" Max asked Leo.

Leo said, "Yeah that would be great."

They exchanged phone numbers and Max asked, "What are you doing in the guy's locker room?"

"We had some questions for the coach." Maggie said. I stared at him hoping he wouldn't ask any more questions.

Leo piped up and said, "I'll call later to schedule a time to study."

"Yeah, sounds good." Max said. We left the locker room, but not before sneaking a quick glance at a very buff guy in nothing, but a g-string.

On our way out, I said to Leo, "Max likes you."

"Like, likes me? As more than friends?" Leo asked.

"Yeah." I said laughing.

"How do you know?"

"I can read minds remember?"

When we were in the parking lot, we saw Leo's roommate. I took the opportunity to ask him where we could find the coach's son. He informed us this was the football stadium, and the coach's son was a football player and we should do the math. We stood outside the locker room, for about fifteen minutes, before the coach's son stepped out of a blue pickup truck. When he got closer to us, Maggie stepped in front of us and with a little flick of her hair she said, "Can we ask you a couple of questions?"

"Sure, what about?" He asked.

"We were wondering if you could tell us about your relationship with Ms. Hayes?" Maggie asked.

"She was the director, for the play I did last year." He said calmly.

"Is that it? You never slept with her? Say, in her office?" Maggie asked him.

"Who told you?" He snapped at us.

"Let's just say an unnamed source." Maggie said.

"This is bullshit! You better not tell anyone!"

"Or what?" Maggie asked.

"I don't know, but I'll think of something."

"Tells us about your relationship. Why would you sleep with an old lady?" Maggie said.

"She wasn't old, and I don't have to tell you anything." He said as he started to walk away.

"Fine, but we have something you will want to know. About your dad and Ms. Hayes." Maggie said.

He stopped, turning to face us. "What is it?"

"I'm not going to tell you, until you tell us first." Maggie said.

"Honestly, there isn't much to tell. I banged her, because she's hot, and she's a teacher. Everything was going fine, until my mom followed me one day to her house and found out about us. My mom was furious, and started threatening Ms. Hayes. The next thing I know, Ms. Hayes is dead. I don't know if my mom killed her, but honestly I find it hard to believe my mom would be strong enough to hang her." He explained. "Now tell me what you know about my dad."

"Well… he was sleeping with Ms. Hayes, too." Maggie said, and immediately started walking really fast back toward campus.

Leo and I quickly started walking after her, while the coach's son yelled after us, "What? What the fuck? That's so gross! You guys better not be lying to me! I will kill you guys, if you are lying to me! That is fucked up!"

Chapter 11

Leo, Maggie and I decided to snoop around the drama stage area to look for the murder weapon. We decided that three sets of eyes were better than one, and even though a lot of people had been on and around the stage since the murder occurred, you never knew what you might find, and it was better to be safe than sorry.

Maggie was wandering up and down each row of seats on her hands and knees to see under all the chairs. I was looking through the technology equipment, the sets and the costumes, Leo was looking on the stage, and the back stage area. Every once and a while you could hear Maggie yell out in pain, as her knee landed on something poky.

I examined every microphone, headset, plastic sword, and paint brush, looking for something that could have made the mark on Ms. Hayes skull, or hoping to find something with blood on it. I was examining the end of a cane, when I heard Leo shout out, "I found something!"

I walked over to the back of the stage, where Leo was lying on his belly, half under the stage. "What is it?" I asked.

Leo started wiggling out from under the stage as Maggie shouted from the seats, "What is it?! I don't want to leave my spot or I'll have to start over!"

"I don't know yet!" I yelled back to her.

Leo stood up and was covered in a thick layer of dust. He handed me a piece of paper. I read what it said:

Dear Sophie Grace Hayes,

> *Your eyes are blue and your hare is red*

> *You make my heart feel like its made of led.*

> *If ran away together, we could be happy*

I'll make this shoret so it won't be sappy.

You look like an angel wen you stand in the lite,

Wen joined together our love can take flite.

Sincerely,

Your Secret Admiror

"Ms. Hayes, had a secret admirer?" I asked to no one in particular.

"What is it?!" Maggie shouted again.

"It's a love letter to Ms. Hayes from her secret admirer!" I yelled to her.

"What?! A love letter?! How did Ms. Hayes get so many guys?!"

I didn't have an answer to her question, so I ignored her. I folded up the letter and put it in my pocket. "Good job finding that Leo! Did you find a weapon under there too?" I asked him.

"No, just some food wrappers and dust. The letter was kind of hidden behind a chip bag."

"Have you found anything yet Maggie?!" I yelled over to her.

"No! There's nothing over here, unless you want some chewed up gum!" Maggie yelled back.

"No! I'm good!" I yelled.

We left the drama stage and went to the dining hall for breakfast. We had to get up early to look around the stage, again, before classes started. The only people who are in the dining hall that early in the morning are the football players. They had already eaten most of the food, so we had to wait a little bit for the cooks to put out more. We saw Max walk by and he said hi to us, but didn't stick around to talk.

Our usual table in the back was open, but it was kind of scary getting there. The football players were big and didn't always see you walking near them. They were loud and sometimes threw things to each other across the room. It was a different experience eating at the dining hall during this time of morning.

The three of us sat down at our table in the back and started talking about Ms. Hayes's love letter.

"Who do you think wrote it, the coach or his son?" Maggie asked.

"Well neither one of them seemed like the romantic type." I said.

"It was a pretty terrible love letter if you ask me." Leo said.

"Well, the letter did say from your 'secret admiror' so I guess it wouldn't be someone she was already in a relationship with and it would be someone who can't spell. Maybe someone less educated who might get over looked."

"Why would anyone sleep with both a son and father? The coach is so old, why sleep with him when you could sleep with the son?" Maggie asked.

"Well we know she was really in love with the coach so maybe sleeping with him full filled some kind of fantasy." I said.

"Yeah, and we know she really wanted to get pregnant, so maybe the coach couldn't get her pregnant and she tried the next best thing, which was his son." Leo said.

"I don't think I would tell them if I was trying to get pregnant because then they might not sleep with me." Maggie said.

"So maybe she didn't tell them about her plan, but maybe the coach had a medical reason he couldn't get her pregnant and she knew about it. She was so in love with him. She wanted a baby with his genes, so she tried getting pregnant by the son." I said.

"I'll see if I can hack into the coach's medical records." Leo said.

"Maybe one of them found out about her plan, got mad and killed her." Maggie said.

"Maybe, but we know the coach's wife found out about the son. I'm betting she's our killer, but she wouldn't have been able to hang the body alone. She had to have had help." I said.

"Maybe the coach or her son was there and helped her out." Leo said.

"How are we going to prove it?" Maggie asked.

"Well, we are going to have to find the murder weapon or get a confession." I said.

"Are we ruling out Mr. Wagner as a murder suspect?" Leo asked.

"I don't think he had any real motive to kill Ms. Hayes. It seems to me that he really loved her, but he made some bad choices in life. I wouldn't be surprised if he is just trying to stay alive, and hide out from the drug dealers." I said.

"What about the school president?" Leo asked.

"He's still a suspect too, but he's less likely. He's old and wouldn't be able to hang her either. We still need to snoop around his office though. You never know where you might find the murder weapon." I said the last part in my best spooky voice.

"Lennox and I will search the president's office, and Leo can look up the coach's medical records." Maggie said.

With the plan laid out, we got up and left the dining hall to get ready for classes.

***

Later in the day Leo obtained the coach's medical records. It revealed that he had a vasectomy about five years earlier. This discovery was the start to proving our theory correct.

While I was in my dorm room working on homework, I got bored and started day dreaming. I was dreaming about visiting Hawaii, when my dream was interrupted by Mr. Wagner. I saw Mr. Wagner in his house, and he was frantically throwing clothes into a suitcase. I heard someone banging on the front door and with every bang Mr. Wagner jumped a little. He grabbed some pants and pulled a couple shirts off the hangers and stuffed them in the suitcase. He grabbed his toothbrush and toothpaste out of the bathroom, and ran down the stairs. He headed straight for the backdoor, when the people at the front door were distracted. I watched him walk along the side of the house with heavy breathing. He peered around the side of the house and looked at the same drug dealers that were after me. The drug dealers were working hard to kick in the front door. When they weren't looking, Mr. Wagner ran down the driveway and down the street. That's when the vision ended, and I came back to the reality of homework.

I had to stop doing homework, to go to my walking class. As part of my major I have to take activity classes. I took a class where you get a grade for walking around campus. Today it was raining, so we had to walk through the library. There were maybe thirty people in my class, and I was trailing behind everyone else. There's no rule on the speed of walking, but the teacher is present to make sure you don't stop. I was on the third floor of the library, when I saw a man at a drinking fountain. He looked like Mr. Wagner. The man was wearing the same clothes, I had seen earlier in my vision. However, the guy's hair was shaggier, and he had more facial hair than Mr. Wagner. I paused as I watched him open a door, and go through it.

I decided to listen to my gut, and follow after him. I opened the door and walked into a stairwell. I guessed he probably went up the stairs, so I did to. The stairs took me to a storage room that looked like the attic. There was the familiar library furniture and some old computers. In the back corner was the man I had seen previously, sitting on a couch and reading a book.

I said quietly, "Mr. Wagner?"

The man jumped up and almost fell over. "It's ok. I'm sorry I scared you. I just want to talk." I said.

He stayed on the other side of the couch. "How do you know who I am?" He asked.

"You're an art teacher on campus, and I know you dated Ms. Hayes. I've been looking into who might have murdered her. I wanted to ask you what you knew."

"I'm hiding. I've got some bad people after me. One of the librarians is in a book club with my mother, and she let me up here."

"You are only hiding from the drug dealers, and not from the police?" I asked.

"Correct. I was in my house the night Sophia was murdered. I wish I had been there, but I was afraid to leave my house. I owe money that I can't pay." He said.

"Do you know who might have wanted her dead?" I asked him.

"The drug dealers have threatened her a few times. Other than them, I can't imagine who would want to hurt her. She was a wonderful woman." He sat back down on his couch and picked up his book.

I took that to mean he was done talking, so I thanked him and left the way I came in. I returned to the second floor. Taking a short cut through the bookshelves I returned to my class as they started their decent to the first floor.

Chapter 12

As I walked out of the library I saw a cheerleader talking to someone at a booth. I quickly darted behind a couple of tall guys, but when they went the opposite way from the dorms, I ducked next to a group of girls. I turned my back away from the cheerleader. Without looking behind me, I walked as fast as I could back to the dorms, while weaving in and out of pedestrians. I was almost to the dining hall, when Maggie called my cell phone.

"Hey Maggie! What's up?" I asked partly out of breath.

"I'm at my sorority house. The girls have been talking about creepy guys that hang out in their parking lot during the night. I was wondering if we could check it out later."

"Yeah, I don't see why not." I said while still power walking to the dorms.

"Why do you sound so out of breath?" Maggie asked me.

"I saw a cheerleader, and I'm practically sprinting back to the dorms."

"Oh, ok. I'll be back in half an hour."

"Ok. Bye." I hung up the phone and sprinted up the stairs, in the dorm. I wasn't going to feel safe, until I was locked in my dorm room.

***

Later that night, Maggie and I got dressed in our superhero personas and drove over to the sorority house. Before we even pulled into the parking lot, I already recognize the guy standing in the parking lot, as a drug dealer.

Maggie shouted, "Damn! It's those drug dealers again! Let's just get out of here!"

"No, I'm tired of these drug dealers. We are going to ask him what he's doing here. It's two against one. We got this Omega girl."

I parked the car and we got out. The drug dealer was wearing a baggy dark sweatshirt and baggy sweatpants. I marched over to him yelling, "What are you doing here? What do you want?"

The guy sauntered over toward me, while holding his pants up. "Yo Bitch! I'm lookin' for you!"

"Well, here I am!" I said while sticking my arms out.

"And know you're going to die!" He said as he whipped out a hand gun.

"Crap!" I thought to myself, as I quickly went to kick the gun out of his hand. The gun went flying into the air, and I sent a second kick to his chest, knocking him backward. An SUV parked across the street started up and began doing a u-turn toward us. I turned around and ran as fast as I could for my car, pushing the button on the remote, to start the ignition. As Maggie and I reached for the door handles, we heard gun shots.

I pulled out of the parking space just as the SUV drove into the driveway. They followed us around the parking lot, before I drove out and switched my car to invisible mode. The drug dealers fired off a couple more shots, in our general direction, before they gave up the search for an invisible car.

"I hate people! Every time my car gets hit with a bullet, I have to fix the paint job! Also, why are the cheerleaders so angry! I didn't mean to knock that girl over!" The more I ranted, the harder I pressed down on the gas pedal.

I was in the middle of a sentence about men, when Leo called to say some guys were in the dorm parking lot harassing women and trying to break into cars.

I sped into the parking lot, almost hitting one of them. I didn't even wait to find a parking spot, before I was out of my car. I wasn't sure where all my anger had come from, but in that moment, I was aggravated and ready to release my fury on anyone, who even remotely irritated me.

The guy I almost hit was wearing a blue shirt. The front was tucked behind his head to reveal a skinny torso. I marched up to him and kicked him in the chest, and punched him in the face. Then I turned around and ran after a guy wearing a white shirt, who was whistling at some girls, as they walked to their car. I came up behind him and put him in a head lock. Maggie ran up behind me and said, "What do you want me to do?"

"Just kick him or hit him or I'm going to ram his head into this car over here!" I shouted at her.

Students from the dorms were starting to congregate along the parking lot. I could hear sirens in the distance, which pissed me off further. I knew I was going to have to leave these guys to the cops, and my mother. With all my strength I twisted the guy in my arms around and rammed his head into a car bumper. I released him, ran to my car for the stun gun and some zip ties.

I chased down the guy in the blue shirt and hit him with the stun gun. Maggie was fighting a guy in a black shirt. I grabbed the blue shirt guy and dragged him to a volleyball court pole and zip tied him. I ran over and stun gunned the guy in the black shirt, while yelling to Maggie, "Don't let the other guy get away!"

Maggie ran after the guy whose head I bashed. He wasn't moving very fast, so it didn't take Maggie much time to grab him. I zip tied the black shirt guy to a tree and ran over and zip tied the red shirt guy to a fence. Maggie and I ran, and got back into our car, as the crowd cheered. I drove back out of the dorm parking lot, so Maggie and I could change out of our superhero costumes, and change the car out of invisible mode.

***

On Saturday our drama class play had its first official dress rehearsal. The person who was supposed to be in charge of all back stage happenings got sick, so I got promoted to backstage manager.

I wasn't sure what I was supposed to be doing. It was chaos. Fortunately, the actors all knew their own costumes and they had people to help them with makeup. I had to make sure everyone got on stage, and that sound and lights were working. I was also in charge of making sure the sets were placed correctly on stage at the right times and that sound and lights were working.

Sky was directing from the front row and watching the performances, when he didn't have to be onstage. I spent most of my time frantically flipping through the play book anticipating what was involved in the next scene, before the current scene ended. I dodged a few sets, and tentatively told an actor to stop talking off stage. Sky hardly noticed me, but I made sure I could see the stage every time he performed.

During the intermission, we had a malfunction with the lights. I helped out by saying to Sky, "um…the lights…the lights don't work." He seemed grateful, although, he didn't actually say anything. He just squinted his eyes at me, like that would help him better understand what I was saying.

During the second half of the play, our lead character lost her wig. It was my job to find it, before her next scene. I ran into everyone's dressing rooms looking for a long blonde wig. I had gotten to the last dressing room when I decided to try a smaller than normal door in the wall. I opened the door to find mops, brooms, cleaning supplies, and walls that were covered in play pamphlets, news paper clippings, love letters and lots of pictures of Ms. Hayes. I suddenly realized that the quiet janitor, who knew a lot about Ms. Hayes affairs, was harboring an unhealthy obsession.

I shut the closet door and calmly walked away. I wasn't sure yet what this new information meant or how it changed things.

I found the blonde wig on top of the wrong actors head, and the show went on. By the end of the day, I felt I had escaped without majorly embarrassing myself in front of Sky, or destroying the production.

Chapter 13

To take a break from dining hall food, Maggie and I had gone to a restaurant. The restaurant was in a poorer part of town. We spotted an SUV that looked similar to the SUV we had seen in the alley. I slowed down a little looking for someone sitting inside, and sure enough, one of the drug dealers, from that night in the alley, was in the car. He didn't see us drive by. I turned onto a side street and put my car in invisible mode. I waited until the SUV drove past and followed it.

The SUV eventually got onto the freeway heading deeper into downtown. We pulled off the freeway into an area with empty buildings and empty lots. There was graffiti decorating every traffic sign and business wall. We followed them to a four story metal warehouse. They drove through a metal gate and parked around the side of the building. It was dark out with only a few lights on the side of the building. I parked my car along the fence, in a spot that gave us a good view of the back of the SUV.

We watched two men get out and open the back of their SUV. They started unloading boxes. The same boxes looked like the ones we found in the van, in the alley. A few more guys holding semi-automatic weapons came out of the warehouse and glanced around. For a moment, I was scared they could see us, but they walked back inside the building. Maggie and I sat there for an hour. We took several pictures with our photo-binoculars. I could see people through the window on the second floor and it looked like they were arguing.

A big side door opened. We could see in to what looked like a chop shop. They drove a nice looking Corvette out, the doors closing behind them. We sat outside for half an hour. Nothing happened, so we decided to go home and come back the next night. I saved the address in my GPS, and drove back to the dorms.

When we got out of the car, Leo was standing in the parking lot talking to Max. Maggie and I walked over to say hi to them.

I said, "Hi Leo. How have you been Max?"

"Good. Thanks for asking." Max said.

"Why are you two talking in the parking lot?" Maggie asked.

"We went to dinner." Leo said.

"Oh that's nice. Maggie and I did too." I said. "We tried calling you, but you didn't answer."

"Wait, you guys went on a date?" Maggie said with excitement.

I felt like I was missing something, so I waited for Leo's answer.

"Yeah, we went on a date. We wanted to go where we wouldn't run into anyone from school. The football team doesn't know Max is gay." Leo answered.

"Well, we will let you two say good night." Maggie said as she shoved me toward the dorms.

***

The next day Maggie and I decided to try and snoop through the school president's office. His name is John Coleman and most students on campus have no idea who he is. He's probably in his sixties and rumors have been circulating that he might retire soon. His office is at the very top floor of the library, and has the best view of the whole campus.

Maggie and I went into the library and got on an elevator. We didn't speak, as the elevator stopped at every floor to let students' off. After the third floor, we were the only ones in the elevator. When the elevator came to a stop the doors opened to reveal nice wood floors, calming lights and a secretary's desk at the end of a short hallway.

We stepped out of the elevator and walked toward a desk. I was hoping I could sneak past the desk, but it sat right between the elevator and Mr. Coleman's office.

Maggie walked up to the secretary and said, "We are here to interview Mr. Coleman, for a school blog, about Ms. Hayes."

"Do you have an appointment?" The secretary asked in a cranky voice. She was wearing a pink cardigan with a gold flower broach on it. She had a white tank top under the cardigan and a high waist black skirt on. Her brown hair was graying, and her nail polish was chipping.

"No, we don't have an appointment. I couldn't get through to anyone, when I tried to call." Maggie said.

"You can't speak with Mr. Coleman, without an appointment." The secretary said authoritatively.

"If he doesn't want to answer questions, he's just going to make himself look guilty." Maggie said.

"Guilty of what?" The secretary asked.

"Of murder." Maggie said as she leaned in closer to the secretary.

"Security!!" The secretary hollered.

I grabbed Maggie's arm briskly walking back to the elevator, pushing the down button a good twenty times. The last thing we needed was to get arrested, or heaven forbid, banned from the library. That could really jeopardize my grade in walking class.

When we got into the elevator, I pushed the button for the second floor.

"Great, what are we going to do know?" Maggie asked.

"We are going to wait for the library to close, and then break into his office."

"Aren't there alarms, or security cameras?" Maggie asked.

"I don't know. We'll find out." I said as we walked off the elevator.

I went to the little door that Mr. Wagner had gone through. Maggie followed me up the stairs and into the storage room. We walked in startling Mr. Wagner, who was sleeping on a couch.

"Hi, Mr. Wagner. We need a place to camp out until the library closes. We think Mr. Coleman might have something to do with Ms. Hayes' death." I said.

"We are going to break into his office. If you hear alarms going off, that's what is happening." Maggie said.

We waited with Mr. Wagner for several hours. He was so excited to have someone to talk to. He practically told us his whole life story. Including the time he was high on something, while camping at a music event in the desert. It involved a conversation with a dragon, while dancing around naked.

Once we saw all the lights getting turned off, we said goodbye to Mr. Wagner. We crept back down the ladder and rode in the elevator to the fourth floor. When we got off, we were relieved to find the secretary's desk empty. I glanced around the ceiling for any security cameras, but didn't see any. We went past the secretary's desk and found the door labeled Mr. Coleman's Office. Maggie picked the lock and we walked in. His office had a desk on the left with a big black padded chair. There were book cases lined with novels, text books, and artifacts. He had two pictures on his desk that looked like they were his wife and grandkids.

Maggie had begun pulling drawers open. I looked around at the objects, to see if any of them could be the murder weapon. After about fifteen minutes of going through papers and objects, including an entire set of golf clubs, we found nothing incriminating. We left the office, and went back to spend the night with Mr. Wagner.

***

Maggie was finally initiated into her sorority. She was so excited about it. I was genuinely happy for her, because I knew how much it meant to her. All of her new sisters were going to the fraternity houses to celebrate. After Maggie spent all day talking me into it, I finally agreed to go with her.

She was thrilled to do my hair and make-up, but I insisted that I leave on my glasses. I wore a flowing blue shirt with beads around the waist, tight jeans, and heels. Maggie wore a white shirt, tucked into a flowery skirt, a jean jacket and wedges. We had even talked Leo into going with us. He wore a black button down shirt and jeans. We walked down the street to the fraternity houses and met up with Maggie's sorority sisters. Greetings and hugs were exchanged by everyone. I felt like I had been friends with them forever, the way they were talking and acting.

We went to a party, in a big two story brick house. We walked through two giant double doors onto wooden floors that were mostly nice, except the occasional sticky spot. The house was full of people, and I didn't recognize anyone. I looked around hoping Sky would be there, but I couldn't see much through all the people. There was hip hop, and rap music blasting from large speakers, making it hard to hear anything people were saying. It didn't bother me, since I can hear what people are thinking, no matter how loud the music gets. I walked around a little and found an ice luge, keg stands, beer pong, and flip cup games. I found the bartender and got myself a drink. I was standing against a wall, when Leo came up to me and grabbed my arm.

Leo yelled into my ear, "Let's dance!"

He pulled me to the dance floor, where I remained for a while. I danced with multiple guys I didn't even know, but I was having fun. I started talking to a girl on the dance floor who wanted a partner for beer pong, so I agreed to play with her. I figured, why not?

I was in the middle of my second round, when Maggie came up and said she needed to talk to me. A girl watching the game offered to take my place, and I stepped over to the side to talk to Maggie.

"There's a guy, who has taken one of my newly initiated sisters into a room. She is super drunk and some of my sisters tried to stop him. He's locked the door, and I need your help getting her out." Maggie said.

"You're the one who can pick locks!" I said while trying to stand still.

"I need you to back me up." Maggie said.

"Ok!" I said.

We weaved our way through people, up a set of big wooden stairs. We went down a hall, took a right, and down another hall. I got totally confused on where we were. There was about ten sorority girls and five fraternity guys standing around door number twenty six.

"Ok, whose room is this?" I asked with one hand on my hip.

"It's the guys', who is in there." A girl with bright red lipstick said.

"Should I pick the lock?" Maggie said.

"Um…wait a minute." I said.

I knocked on the door three times and waited a second for a response. Then I turned around to face the crowd of people and shouted. "Ok, I know one of you fraternity guys has a fucking key to this room! I don't care if that's your fucking fraternity brother in there! You are going to fucking open this door! Fucking lock picking ruins locks, so you would have to fucking replace the lock, or I could fucking kick the door down! It's your fucking choice guys! You want to magically produce a key, to this fucking room, so I can fucking stop a girl from getting raped? Or do you fucking want a lawsuit, on your fucking hands?" I had my hands flying around in the air and my hip jutted to the side. I was slightly bent over, and then bent back, as I shouted out my rants. "Nobody wants to hand over a key? Fine!" I lifted my foot and placed it against the door, backing up and putting my fists up.

I was about to run at the door, when a guy shouted, "Wait! I have a key!"

He walked out of the crowd and opened the door. All the girls rushed into the room, to find the girl passed out on the bed, with her shirt and bra off. Several girls hit the guy, and one kicked him in the nuts. They scooped the girl up and walked out of the room. On their way out they thanked me, and told me how cool I was. I was relieved my rant worked, because I was pretty sure I wasn't actually able to kick the door down. The fraternity guys pulled the guy out of the room and one older looking guy, holding a paddle, took the guy by the arm. They walked him down the hall saying, "That's not how we treat the women that walk into this house…"

Maggie said to me, "I could have just picked the lock."

"I wanted to try something new." I said. We went and found Leo, thoroughly enjoying himself on the dance floor. We dragged a reluctant Leo out of the house, and stumbled our way back to the dorms.

***

The next day in the afternoon, we went with Leo to watch a football scrimmage. It was surprisingly boring. I couldn't even make it fun by guessing which player had the best butt. When the scrimmage was over, Leo, Maggie and I walked to my car discussing what we could do later that night. To the surprise of Maggie and me, Leo really wanted to go with us to investigate the ware house.

"I've been taking kick boxing classes, and I want to be a part of the action! I think I could be helpful." Leo said.

"Alright then, would you two like to go now? If we go before dark, we might be able to get to the ware house when it's empty." I said.

"Let's do this!" Maggie said.

Leo and I gave her a look and climbing into the car without saying anything. I drove to the warehouse putting the car in invisible mode. I parked and we surveyed the scene. There was a guy outside a side door smoking, but other than that it looked kind of empty and quiet. We walked through the gate staying low, along the fence line. There were bushes along the fence line, which we used as a shield. We had brought various devices with us, to collect evidence, and to protect ourselves. I personally was very annoyed with these drug dealers shooting at me, and I was ready to go into the warehouse with my own personal vendetta.

"I don't see anyone inside. Are you guys ready to make a run for the building?" Maggie said.

"Lets run to that second window, from the right. I think we should check all the windows, before trying to enter." I said.

The guy who had been smoking, walked back inside. We ran, staying low to the ground, until we got to the second window to the right. We crouched down below the window, I pulled a small scope from my pocket. I expanded the scope and lifted it to right below the window sill. I looked through the view screen and saw a room with a table and a chair.

"There's nothing in this room." I said.

We crawled along the wall, keeping an eye on the rest of the yard. I used my scope through the next window and saw a room full of boxes and an open door revealing a hallway. We crawled to the next window and found three men talking to each other around a big wooden desk. I pulled out a listening device and turned it on.

One man said, "We have some sellers coming by to pick up some weed. Do we have any in stock?"

Another man said, "Yeah. It's in the room down the hall. Are these the kids from the college?"

The first man said, "Yes."

The second man said, "See if you can talk them into selling some Xanex and Speed for us, too."

A third man said, "The gun order won't come in until tomorrow. Our distributer got held up at the border."

The second man said, "What kind of operation are we running here? I have a buyer coming by later to talk about guns that we don't have? Get out of my office!"

It got quiet after we heard a door shut, so we kept crawling along the wall. At the next window we saw a wide open area with cars, boxes, crates, and barrels. When we were done looking through windows, we discussed how we were going to break in. It didn't look like there were many people inside, but I thought of a way to get to the roof. Maggie and Leo decided to wait near the door where the smoker had come through. I attached one of my ropes to the gutter and climbed the side wall, where there were no windows. Once I was on the roof, I found a door. It was locked. I walked around trying to think of another way in, when I got called on my walky talky.

"Koko, there is an open window on the third floor, on the north side."

I walked to the north side pulling out the scope. Lowering to the open window, I saw an empty room with an open door leading to a balcony over the main floor. The room had nothing in it, so I used my ropes to lower myself onto the window sill and crawl in. I walked as quietly, as I could, over to the open door. I listened for any talking and heard two men talking down on the main floor. I placed my scope down low to the floor. I couldn't see the men talking. I walked along the balcony hallway staying close to the wall.

Every time I came to an open room I used the scope to check it, before proceeding. I found a stair well and walked down to the second floor. I checked for the location of people on the main floor, before continuing down the stairs. I got to the bottom and crouched down behind a big brown box. Using objects to hide me, I crouched to the door, where Maggie and Leo were waiting. I quietly opened the door and radioed to Maggie and Leo to come around the corner.

When we were all inside, we walked to the room with the boxes. I heard someone walk into the ware house and crouched behind a car.

One man said, "I want some cocaine. I have several sellers, who are getting a lot of questions about buying cocaine."

I pulled my tape recorder from my pocket and turned it on.

The second man said, "How much do you want?"

"two kilos for now. We will see how it sells."

"Alright. Walk with me. We have some down the hall." That's when I realized he was walking in my direction. I crawled under the car and walky talkied Maggie and Leo to tell them what was happening. They had already split up. Leo was in a room with several packets of pills. Maggie was watching a drug exchange, outside the building. The two men walked past me. Once they were out of sight, I slid out from under the car.

I met up with Maggie and Leo on the second floor where we discussed an exit strategy. I was talking about getting all of us out the door Maggie and Leo had used to come in, when I heard a familiar voice. I looked over the banister to see a male cheerleader and three female cheerleaders, including the one I had bumped into. They shouted at a drug dealer, "Where is she? The blonde. We know she is here somewhere, we put a tracking device on her car. Is her car one of these cars? Where is she?"

"Crap! The cheerleaders found me!" I whispered. "We need to get out of here ASAP."

More drug dealers and drug sellers were coming into the warehouse. I was getting nervous about us being discovered. The drug dealer talking to the cheerleaders said, "I don't know who you guys are talking about, but if you don't get out, we will force you out in a body bag."

"I'm not afraid of you. I'm not leaving here, until I have the blonde."

The drug dealer yelled, "Boss!! We have a situation out here!" Five guys walked out holding guns. I was about to tell Maggie and Leo to make a run for the stairs, when I heard a man's voice coming from behind us.

He yelled, "Intruders! There are intruders!"

Maggie was standing closest to him and she punched him in the throat. He gagged and stumbled backward. The three of us ran for the stairs. A guy was running up the stairs, Leo ran into him, knocking him down the stairs. The cheerleaders had multiplied and were running around the warehouse in search of "the blonde". Drug dealers were running around trying to catch cheerleaders, and stop the three of us from leaving the building. Leo was almost to the door, when a guy ran at him and tackled him to the ground. I tried kicking him, while pulling out my stun gun, but two more guys grabbed my arms. I was able to free myself from one, but the other increased his grip on my arm, which looked small in his large hand. I tried kicking him in the groin, but I was hit in the head and lost consciousness.

When I came to, I was strapped to a chair with duck tape over my mouth. I was sitting in a room by myself, but the door was open and I could see some of what was happening. About twenty guys were fighting and shooting cheerleaders who were running around, flipping off cars, flying through the air, and doing an impressive job of fighting the drug dealers. I didn't see Maggie and Leo, but I was hoping they were ok.

A guy with a gun walked into my room, and aimed the gun at my head. I was surprisingly calm. I thought to myself, "Ok, now is the time I'm going to die."

The man said, "You and your partner caused us to lose a lot of drug money! My boss isn't happy. I'm not going to kill you. My boss wants your head himself. He's going to make an example out of you."

It was hard to hear him talking with all the yelling and gun shots going off. I was trying to get my hands loose, when I saw Maggie peak around a corner followed by Leo. The two crept up behind the man holding the gun; Leo grabbed the gun pointing it toward the rough. Maggie kicked the guy between the legs, and then stunned him. He fell to the ground. Maggie tied him up and Leo cut me loose.

We ran out of the room and down the hall. I saw a couple drug dealers lying on the ground, either unconscious, tied up or both. There were also a couple cheerleaders lying on the ground bleeding. I wanted to help them, but my own life was at stake.

Leo cried out in pain, and I turned to see him bleeding from the arm. A guy ran over and grabbed Maggie. She yelled at me, "Run!"

I hesitated, trying to decide if I should stay and help, or run and save myself. In that moment I heard a loud crash, and turned around to see a line of swat team members enter the building. More guns were getting fired. I crouched down to avoid getting hit, when someone grabbed me. I wiggled loose and started running. The guy chased me all the way up the stairs. I ran to the roof, because I wasn't sure where else to go. I stopped and got ready to fight the man. It was dark, pouring down rain and the wind had picked up.

I kicked and punched. He deflected and punched me back. We moved closer to the edge with every jab and kick. When I reached the ledge I stopped. The man grabbed me around the throat. "I am going to take your life in exchange for the money I lost, when you interrupted my drug deal."

His fingers were tightening on my throat and his body weight was pinning me in a very uncomfortable position against the roof. His hair was thinning and his breath smelled. Again I thought to myself, "I'm dying now."

My vision was getting blurry and my lungs were burning. I desperately tried kicking at him, pulling his fingers back from my throat or even squeezing a pressure point on his wrist. I was losing consciousness when a thick arm wrapped itself around the guy's neck and yanked him back. I gasped for air and watched the Crimson Eagle kick and punch the guy, until he was knocked out.

The Crimson Eagle said, "I was flying by looking for crime, when I saw you up here. What are you doing here?"

"I was investigating some illegal activity, when some cheerleaders showed up and the drug dealers found us. Thanks for saving my life." I said.

"No problem babe. Are there more people here who need help?"

"Yeah, Omega girl, the Blue Sleuth and a bunch of hurt cheerleaders. You have to go through a window or ground level door. The door up here is locked from the outside."

"You want a lift down then?"

"No, I have my rope. I can do it myself. Hey, why don't you wear a cape? It would make it easier to spot you coming."

"Too much wind resistance."

The Crimson Eagle leaped off the roof and gracefully flew to the ground. I attached a rope to a wet gutter and propelled down. I was almost to the bottom, when a gust of wind blew me sideways and my foot slipped on the wet surface. I got tied up in the rope and was dangling upside down against the wall in the pouring rain.

The Crimson Eagle rushed over and said, "Are you ok? How can I help?"

"Um, well, maybe try and get my foot untangled." I said.

He reached up and tried untangling my foot. When he got my foot loose he was standing less than a centimeter away from me and it was making my heart race a little. He said, "What now?"

I said, "Help me flip around."

He put his hands on my waist and looked into my eyes. I was having trouble breathing through my nose in the rain, so I had my mouth slightly open. We locked eyes and he leaned in and kissed me. It was a gentle kiss full of passion. His hands moved up and down my waist as the kiss got stronger. He pulled slightly away and pushed me up, so I could flip around. I finished lowering myself and said, "We should check on the others."

We ran into the building and saw Leo and Maggie hiding behind a car. I also saw my mom shooting at a drug dealer. The Crimson Eagle and I crawled over to them. I said, "Go with the Crimson Eagle. He will help you guys get out. Leo you go first." The two of them started weaving their way through the warehouse, trying to avoid flying bullets. I saw a cheerleader crouched in fear behind a box. I motioned for her to come over. She quickly crawled over to us. "Omega girl will help you get to the door." I said to her.

The two of them started crawling the same way the Crimson Eagle and Leo had gone. I was waiting for my opportunity to start crawling back, when a drug dealer rolled in next to me, to hide from the gun shots. He looked at me, and I looked at him, not sure what to do. He suddenly smiled and stuck the gun to my head. He said, "Get up." I stood up and turned around to face the majority of the action. He said, "Walk." I walked out toward the gun shooting.

The shooting had mostly stopped, because the police were gaining an upper hand on the drug dealers. The guy with the gun to my head said, "I've got the bitch! Where's the boss?"

A guy stood up and said, "He's not here. I get second dibs." He raised his gun and took aim at me. He pulled the trigger at the same time my mom came out of nowhere, jumping in front of me. The police shot both guys; the one holding a gun to my head and the one shooting at me.

My mom fell to the floor with blood oozing out of her chest. "No!" I yelled. I crouched down and applied pressure. Several officers ran over to help me stop the bleeding, but my mom said, "Give us a minute." As she waived the officers away.

"I'm sorry mom." I whispered to her. All of my anger I felt toward her over the years was gone. I felt sad I never had gotten to know her or had gotten an opportunity at a typical mother-daughter relationship.

People were being hauled out in handcuffs and body bags. I saw more blood coming out of her back and her abdomen. She took a breath of air and said, "I'm proud of who you have become." She let out a breath of air and her whole body relaxed. I sat on the ground letting my pants get soaked by her blood. I wasn't ready to admit to myself she was dead. She died protecting me. That warranted forgiveness for not being around, while I grew up. Some EMT's came and checked for a pulse. They shook their heads and pulled out a body bag. I felt tears drip down my face, as I looked around at the scene of blood and bullet holes surrounding the warehouse.

How did everything get so out of hand? How could I have let so many people die? Why couldn't I even protect my own family?

I felt a hand on my shoulder as my mom was wheeled away on a stretcher. I looked up and saw the Crimson Eagle, Maggie and Leo standing behind me.

"Are you ok?" Maggie asked.

I wiped a tear off my face, and stood up. I said, "I will be."

We walked out of the building together and handed all of our evidence over to the police. I also informed them that the "boss" was stuck on the roof. On our way to the car, I started to shake, and my teeth started to chatter. I wasn't sure how much of it was from the cold, and how much was from the stress of the night's events.

Maggie said in a soft concerned voice to me, "I better drive."

***

The next day I woke up more determined than ever to solve Ms. Hayes murder. I had a strong feeling the answers were going to be found with the janitor. Before I could look through the janitor's house, I had to go to class. Nobody was teaching many classes that day, because the whole campus was morning the loss of five cheerleaders. There were candles, pictures, and ribbons decorating the campus in their honor.

In the evening, we knew the janitor would be working on campus. His house would be empty. Maggie, Leo and I drove to his address. He lived in an apartment complex, in a large brick building. We pushed the buttons next to people's names until someone opened the door, to let us in. We walked up some questionable stairs to the third floor and found his apartment door labeled 3E. Maggie picked the lock. We went inside. It was cluttered and dirty with newspapers and trash littered everywhere.

"For being a janitor, he's not very clean." Leo said.

"Maybe, after cleaning all day, he wants to come home and…not clean." Maggie said.

"Look for a blunt force object with blood on it." I said to them both. I caught Maggie rolling her eyes, but she started looking around the apartment. I scoured through the kitchen, determined to find proof that he was our killer. I pulled drawers out and examined every kitchen tool. After going through the fourth drawer, I sat down at the kitchen table. I was grasping at straws. I needed to think about what happened that night on the drama stage.

First the coach's wife was arguing with Ms. Hayes, and then the janitor said he saw a cheerleader show up. I knew the janitor had written Ms. Hayes a love letter, but she either didn't like it or she never received it. Ms. Hayes was trying to blackmail the school president, and was sleeping with both the football coach and his son. The drug dealers wanted her boyfriend. I felt like there was something else. What was I forgetting? Oh, Ryan, the student Ms. Hayes was sleeping with!

I didn't know how Ryan was involved or why the cheerleader was on the drama stage, the night Ms. Hayes died. Either one of them could have been the killer or linked to the killer. Since we were in the janitor's house, we needed to rule him out as a suspect.

If I was going to give someone a love letter, what else might I have with me? Flowers? A present? I got up from the table and looked around the kitchen for a flower vase. I found one in the cupboard, but it couldn't have made the dent on Ms. Hayes' head. I went into the bedroom and looked for a present, but didn't see anything.

"Have you guys found anything yet?" I asked Leo and Maggie.

"I found a nice pair of loafers." Leo said.

"I found nothing. There's just a lot of junk." Maggie said.

"I think we might need to call the Crimson Eagle. I have two suspects we haven't checked out yet, but I don't know who they are." I said.

"What makes you think the Crimson Eagle will?" Maggie asked.

"He has connections, we can use in the police department." I said.

"Ok, let's call him. Do you have the number for that phone you gave him?" Maggie said.

"Yes, it's in my car."

We walked back down to the car and I called the Crimson Eagle.

"Yo. Crimson Eagle here."

"Yo, it's Koko." I said mocking him. "Don't make a big deal out of this, but I need your help."

"What do you need?" He asked.

"I have two suspects in the murder, and no way of figuring out who they are. I have no idea who murdered Ms. Hayes, and I'm running out of places to turn." I said.

"Well, you have called the right superhero. I just finished talking to the police. Ms. Hayes was sleeping with a Chris Coleman and a Ryan Stewart, who are both students at school."

"Did they mention anything about a cheerleader or the football coach?" I asked.

"They didn't say anything about them to me."

"Ok, meet us at the theater on campus." I said.

I hung up the phone and drove to campus. "Leo, I need you to use my computer here in the car to look up a Ryan Stewart. I'm going to go inside the theater by myself, and see if Ms. Hayes will send me a vision from the night she was murdered. I'm desperate for an answer."

I walked into the theater and went to the side of the stage. I tried relaxing and clearing my head. It's easier said than done, and it took me a few minutes to do. I heard talking behind me. When I turned around I was excited to see Ms. Hayes talking to the coach's wife.

Ms. Hayes yelled, "I will not confess to anything, but if you are so certain that I'm sleeping with your son, maybe you should do something about it!"

Mrs. Clark said, "Maybe I will!" She walked off the stage and out the door.

Ms. Hayes was standing on the stage, when a cheerleader walked over to her and tentatively said, "Ms. Hayes? I was wondering if I could ask you something?"

Ms. Hayes responded with a smile, "Yes dear, what is it?"

"I was wondering if you thought I had a chance at trying out for a main character in the upcoming play. I tried out last year and didn't get any parts. I don't want to audition again this year if I'm that bad at acting."

"Darling, you are not a bad actor. You just weren't what we were looking for in last year's play. That shouldn't discourage you from trying out for this year's play. You just might be exactly what we are looking for!"

"Ok, thanks Ms. Hayes." The cheerleader said and walked off the stage.

I few moments passed as Ms. Hayes stood on the stage walking back and forth and muttering to herself. I saw the janitor holding a small piece of paper and dressed in a brown suit. He was standing off to the corner of the stage looking at the paper and reciting whatever was written on it.

The janitor walked up to her and said, "Uh, Sophia? I wroted you a letter. I wanta read it to ya'."

Ms. Hayes stopped and walked toward him. "Alright Hank, what is it?"

He read her his poem and she said, "Oh, Hank that was a very lovely poem. Thank you."

She started walking off the stage, but the janitor said, "Wait! It's a love poem."

"I know." She said.

"But I love ya." Hank said.

"Hank, you couldn't possibly love me. You don't know me."

"But, I see ya every day and you say hi tu me. Nobody else says hi tu me. You're so b'utiful, and I want tu marry you."

Ms. Hayes was about to let him down softly when Ryan walked on stage. Ryan said, "You don't love her, nobody loves her. She just uses people."

Ryan looked angry as he walked toward Ms. Hayes. Ms. Hayes said, "Hank, please, just get out of here. We can talk later."

The janitor turned around and walked off the stage, disappearing into the back.

Ryan said, "I slept with you to get a good grade in this class. Without an A I can't graduate. You gave me a C on the last test. What's up with that?"

Ms. Hayes said, "Ryan, people will get suspicious, if I give you A's and your work is all wrong. It would help if you actually studied, and tried to do well. I can bump your grade up a little at the end."

"Is that what you are doing for Chris Coleman? Bumping his grade up?" Ryan said.

"Yes, but he actually studies."

"Studying wasn't in our agreement!" Ryan said.

"Ryan we didn't really have an agreement. The first time we slept together, it just kind of happened. After that I told you I would be able to help you pass the class."

At this point, Hank had returned to the stage holding a trash grabber. He walked quickly toward Ryan holding out the trash grabber like a lacrosse stick.

"What the hell man?" Ryan said at seeing Hank.

"Hank! Put that down!" Ms. Hayes said.

"He don't treat ya' like a woman!" Hank said.

Hank lunged at Ryan, pushing Ryan pack with the trash grabber. Ryan lunged forward at Hank and punched him in the eye. Hank stumbled back and Ms. Hayes tried getting in between them.

"Stop! Both of you!" Ms. Hayes said.

Hank swung the trash grabber at Ryan's head, but Ryan ducked. Hank's momentum hit Ms. Hayes instead. Ms. Hayes fell to the ground and didn't move.

Ryan and Hank looked at each other and both started panicking. Ryan was pacing back and forth saying, "She can't be dead, she can't be dead. I have to graduate! I can't go to jail!"

Hank was on his hands and knees, shaking Ms. Hayes trying to get her to wake up and he was starting to cry.

Ryan bent down and checked for her pulse. Then he looked at Hank and said, "I have an idea. Let's make it look like a suicide. There's some rope in the back we use to pull set designs. We can make a noose and hang her from it. The police will think she committed suicide. It's perfect."

Ryan ran to get the rope. Hank shakily lifted Ms. Hayes up while brushing her hair out of her face. It took Ryan a few tries to get the rope over the catwalk. They got Ms. Hayes into the noose, and anchored the rope down.

Ryan said to Hank, "Not a word of this to anyone, or I'll come back and slit your throat!"

Ryan walked off the stage and the vision went away. I ran to the janitor's closet and found the trash grabber. I called the police to let them know, I found the murder weapon. I told them that Ryan and Hank were the murderers.

I walked back outside and found Maggie and Leo cheering.

"We heard on the police scanner, that you solved Ms. Hayes murder!" Leo said.

"We solved Ms. Hayes murder." I corrected them. "I couldn't have done it without you guys."

"Group hug!" Maggie said while putting her arms out.

I didn't even hesitate. I went right in for a group hug.

***

The next day we had the official opening of the drama play, which was being dedicated to Ms. Hayes. The play was scheduled for the evening. Since I did such a good job as the backstage manager the first time, they let me do it again for opening night.

Before I started my duties for the play, there was one thing we all had to do first. Meet the new police chief. His name was Brian Adams. He wanted to have a good relationship with all the crime fighters in town, by meeting all of us personally. When Maggie, Leo and I walked into the police station, we were met by cheers and 'congratulations'. It was nice to be appreciated by the police force.

The chief was a nice man with graying hair and an intense interest in what I do. He seemed nice enough. I saw good things in our future working relationship.

On our way through the lobby of the police station, we saw Mr. Wagner. He was turning himself in for selling drugs. The future appeared in a vision. I saw the police giving him a light sentence, in exchange for him testifying against the drug dealers.

Before we left the building, I asked the police chief, "Are they going to be hard on the janitor? Killing Ms. Hayes was an accident."

"I think he will get away with a light sentence, if he is even charged with murder at all." Adams said.

"Well, it was nice to meet you. I look forward to working with you." I shook his hand and walked out the door.

I was half way through the door, when I saw the Crimson Eagle coming up the steps. "Are you here to see the police chief?" I asked him.

"Yeah, I don't have much time. I'm running late for an event I have this evening." He said.

He bent down to kiss me and I noticed he had a black eye. "Did you get punched?" I asked him.

"Yeah, this chick trying to rob a clothing store in the mall put up a huge fight. I heard you found the murderer in the drama teacher case? Congratulations."

"Thanks..." I didn't finish my sentence because Leo flung the police station door open and it hit me right in the face. I stumbled backward and everyone laughed as I fell into a bush along the police station wall.

Maggie reached down, and helped me out of the bush. I was left with a lot of cuts down my arms.

"I'm so sorry!" Leo said.

"Don't worry about it." I said. "We should really get going."

I kissed the Crimson Eagle good bye and we took off for the play.

When we got to the drama stage everyone was going crazy, because Sky wasn't there yet. I put my head set on and started barking out orders. I was finding costumes, fixing lights, sweeping aisles ways and running lines with people. We were fifteen minutes from starting, when Sky came barreling in from the side doors. He shouted to everyone, "I'm so sorry. I got held up! Let's have a great show tonight people!"

I was standing next to the stage waiting for the actors to get ready to go on. Sky walks up to me and watches a couple guys arrange the props on stage. I look up at him and see he has a black eye. Exactly like the one the Crimson Eagle had.

I put my hands on my hips, turned to face him and said, "Crimson Eagle."

He looked down at me a little startled and stared for a few moments unsure of what to say. He noticed the cuts on my arms, smiled and said, "Koko."

Made in the USA
San Bernardino, CA
06 January 2014